ATTACK
Of The
CUPIDS

★ A MUDDLE & WIN MISSION ★

Also by John Dickinson

Muddle and Win: The Battle for Sally Jones
The Cup of the World
The Widow and the King
The Fatal Child
The Lightstep
W.E.

JOHN DICKINSON

ATTACK OF THE CUPIDS

A MUDDLE & WIN MISSION

David Fickling Books

OXFORD · NEW YORK

31 Beaumont Street
Oxford OX1 2NP, UK

ATTACK OF THE CUPIDS
A DAVID FICKLING BOOK 978 0 857 56089 6

Published in Great Britain by David Fickling Books,
a division of Random House Children's Publishers UK
A Random House Group Company

This edition published 2013

1 3 5 7 9 10 8 6 4 2

The Random House Group Limited supports the Forest Stewardship Council
(FSC©), the leading international forest-certification organisation. Our books
carrying the FSC label are printed on FSC©-certified paper. FSC is the only
forest-certification scheme supported by the leading environmental organisations,
including Greenpeace. Our paper procurement policy can be found at
www.randomhouse.co.uk/environment

Set in 12/16pt Goudy Old Style

DAVID FICKLING BOOKS
31 Beaumont Street, Oxford, OX1 2NP

www.randomhousechildrens.co.uk
www.totallyrandombooks.co.uk
www.randomhouse.co.uk

Addresses for companies within The Random House Group Limited can be
found at: www.randomhouse.co.uk/offices.htm

THE RANDOM HOUSE GROUP Limited Reg. No. 954009

A CIP catalogue record for this book is available from the British Library.

Printed and bound in Great Britain by Clays Ltd, St Ives plc

1: THE END OF THE WORLD

The world is about to end.

The world is always about to end. For thousands of years, everyone has known it was going to happen.

Some have said it would be destroyed by fire. Some have said it would be flood. Some have said it would be fire *and* flood (and, of course, quite a lot of steam too). The Ancient Persians thought a great lizard would wake and ravage all the lands. The Vikings believed there would be a winter of three years followed by a great battle between gods and giants in which the Earth would get wiped out just because it was in the way. And the Aztecs said that there would be a huge earthquake and the sun would fall from the sky and That Would Be It – for the fifth time, because they also believed the world had ended four times already.

In modern times gods and giant lizards have gone out of fashion. People prefer to think of scientific reasons why everything should go pop. Nuclear war was a good one. You couldn't get more scientific than a nuclear war. Although, strangely, all those old ideas about battle and fire and everlasting winter were still going to be part of it somehow.

Then someone noticed how much everyone depended on computers these days and suggested that all the computers would suddenly stop working on the stroke of midnight. And that, of course, would be the end of absolutely everything.

Then somebody else noticed how much carbon humans were pumping into the atmosphere, and after quite a lot of complicated science people started to worry about floods and everlasting winter all over again.

Year in, year out, through the whole of history, people have been expecting the end of the world. Especially in years with lots of zeros.

And they have all been right. All of them.

(Except the Aztecs, who were on something they shouldn't.)

The world really is about to end.

It always has been.

High above the clouds, in one of the thousand wings of the palaces of Heaven, there is a room.

Visitors – should there be any – reach it by passing down a long corridor. The passage walls are built of Sorrow and the floor is paved with Deep Cold. The light is – well – *thicker*, more colourful than it should be, and the further you go the thicker and more colourful it gets, until it seems almost solid, pressing upon the skin. An ominous groaning fills the air.

At the end there is a door made of human tears. Beside it is written in letters of fire:

DEPARTMENT OF GEOGRAPHY

Oops.

(Is this the right place?)

(All right, maybe it is the right place. But should we be here?)

Swallow hard. Open the door, gently. The sounds of groaning increase. They're coming from all around – from a million million throats, which have not yet groaned these groans, but when they do they will groan them so terribly that you can already hear them, now, in this chamber of stillness surrounded by walls of wind.

The winds spiral up and up. They form the shape of a vast beehive, closing at last in a purple dome far overhead. All the space within them is filled with bookcases – bookcases as tall as cathedrals, running left, running right, away into infinity. And every shelf is packed with folders that have titles like *Ragnarök* and *Great Plague*, *Armageddon* and *Apocalypse 2012* and *Pole Shift* and *Galactic Alignment*, on and on, one after another, pages and pages and pages. Each page has been spun from someone's dying breath, and every one describes, calmly and carefully, how the world will end. They are all different. Although they do repeat each other quite a lot.

In this stillness, in this unending library of destruction, something moves. A figure like the shadow of a small eclipse, huge and silent, stalks between the shelves. The groaning of as-yet-unslain souls weaves itself in a comet-trail behind him. Robed in fire, shod in flood, he comes. Darkness is on his brow, sickness on his breath, his wings are thunderclouds and his eyes white ice. He is the Archangel Destruction, the Herald of Calamity – the One, who, at the Final Word, shall have the sorrowful task of showing the human race its chequered flag. He has many names. Some call him Azreal. Some call him Thanatos, some call him Grimnir, some Ankou. Quite a lot of people call him 'Sir' or 'My Lord', especially when they meet him.

But when his back is turned?

Well, then it's a different story. The seraphs who bow before him pull faces and jerk their thumbs if they think he's not looking. The angels who greet his coming with halleluiahs burst into fits of giggles as soon as he's passed. He knows it. The reason he looks so stony-faced is not because he is supposed to end billions of human lives. It's because he's trying not to notice that the choir has got the hiccups again.

He knows what they call him too. It's 'Daddy Doomsday'.

In some ways Heaven is like everywhere else. You can be as majestic as you like, as creative, as powerful, as brilliant; but if everything you do ends in failure, too bad. You just don't get the respect.

Doomsday's eye roams the shelves. He reads the names on the folders. He remembers every one. *The Babel Project* – ah yes, very neat. There had been something poetic in using mankind's greatest achievement (speech) to sow the seeds of mankind's destruction. When they had told him it must go no further, he had almost cried.

The Great Plague 171ˢᵗ edition. Easy and effective. You could always rely on a Great Plague. Except that you never had to.

Enormous Aardvark Eats the Sun.

Aha. Ahem. That one, he had to admit, had been a little on the flaky side. His staff had put it together at a time when three of their very best Ends of the World had just been cancelled one after another. Everyone had been upset. Of course it was really a protest. He shouldn't have let it go, but he had. It had earned him an icy memo from the Governors.

In its *elements*, it should have been acceptable. Something eating the Sun was an idea they had used many times. The aardvark was a holy beast to . . . some human tribe or other, he couldn't quite remember which one. And the flood was perfectly standard as well.

Although it shouldn't really have been a flood of aardvark puke. He ought to have known that would cause trouble.

'Sir.'

Doomsday turned. A smart young angel, clothed in white light, was looking up at him.

An effort of memory. 'Ah. Mishamh.'

He managed not to make the name sound like a question. Mishamh was one of his assistants, on loan from the Physics Department. He did know that. But like anyone else who had been around since The Beginning, he had a lot to remember. He *could* remember it all. It was just that sorting through it took a while.

'It's ready, sir.'

The angel held up a folder. Its title was:

ASTEROID (38562975) Zebukun

Doomsday took it. He turned the pages slowly. He always showed respect for the work of a colleague – however junior – and for the souls upon whose final breaths the work had been written.

It was good. It planned for all of the things that were supposed to happen on the Last Day. And it was perfectly clear – which was unusual for anything written by the Physics staff, who normally used words that no one else understood and sentences that had been dragged through a black hole backwards.

'Not bad,' he said. 'Really not bad at all.'

The angel looked at him hopefully. He was expecting questions. Doomsday tried to think of one.

'Time to impact?'

'Six months, sir. It's on page one.'

So it was. Exactly on the deadline that the Governors had passed down to him.

'Very good.'

'I've got the flood in, sir,' said the angel, who was rocking a bit as he stood, as if he wanted to hop from foot to foot in his eagerness. 'Section fourteen – the impact's in the northern ocean, sending a great wave around the world. And the fault lines fracture, sir, so we get the fire – that's the magma coming up from below. And in the appendices there's an option on everlasting winter – we'd need a go or no-go decision on that by Month Minus Four . . .'

'Excellent,' said Doomsday carefully. 'A nod to tradition. I like that.'

Doomsday knew his assistants thought he was hopelessly old-fashioned (or maybe, just hopelessly old). He did not mind. He made up old-fashioned things to say, said them, and then carefully looked somewhere else so that the lads could roll their eyes and jerk their thumbs behind his back. He did it to humour them. Working on the things they did, they needed all the humouring they could get.

He *did* have likes and dislikes. He did not, personally, like asteroids. He felt that the end of the world ought to come from within the world itself. The seeds of destruction should have been there from the very beginning. That was why he preferred projects such as Babel and the Millennium Bug. They were neat. The way they finished things off gave meaning to everything that had gone before. It was difficult to find meaning in a random splat.

But he did not let his feelings get in the way of his work.

'Good job. You may put it to the Governors.'

'Do you think they'll go for it, sir?' Mishamh *was* hopping from foot to foot now. 'Do you think they will?'

Doomsday looked at his colleague thoughtfully.

The lad was very young. He couldn't have been more than a century – there was still down on his feathers. He worked surrounded by failed plans for the end of the world, and if he thought anything about them it was that somehow each and every one, in some detail, could not have been good enough. He knew there was no flaw in his own plan. It was simple, and at the same time it had everything. He really thought he had done it. He had found the one piece that had been missing from the Great Curriculum all this time.

He had as much understanding of Heaven as a fly has of spiders' webs.

'Come with me,' said Doomsday, in a voice that was not unkindly.

He led Mishamh down the aisles between the shelves. Together, they passed through the Door of Tears. They strode along the Passage of Ice, adjusting their pace easily as the floor rose and fell beneath them. (The floor rose and fell because the Geography Department was in a wing of the Heavenly palaces. When you ask the Heavenly Architects to put a 'wing' on a building in the sky they think you really mean it.)

'Uh – where are we going, sir?'

'The Appeals Board.'

Mishamh was young, but he knew better than to ask why. It's not a question that gets asked in Heaven. To ask 'Why' is to ask why love has allowed pain, why order has led to chaos, why perfection has given life to imperfection. It is to probe into the mysteries of the

Great Curriculum itself. If you dare to ask the question 'Why?' you are going to have to listen to a very long answer. If you're lucky.

If you're *unlucky*, you might be listening to a very short one.

Down below them, small and blue and beautiful, turned the world they were going to destroy.

2: SALLY AT A WINDOW

'Not bad,' said Mr Kingsley. 'Really not bad at all.'

Tuesday morning, Classroom C23, Darlington High School. Mr Kingsley's words were as soft as snowflakes and there was a shiver in them that was as close as he ever came to delight.

Sally waited.

The period was over. Everyone else had gone, stuffing their books into their bags and hurrying out into the corridors to make the most of morning break. But Sally had already finished her essay in class, so she had handed it in to Mr Kingsley before leaving. And Mr Kingsley had begun to mark it at once. She could have left him to get on with it but he had seemed to expect her to stay. So she had.

'Hm,' said Mr Kingsley. He squiggled a line in

green ink. Mr Kingsley always used green.

Outside the sky was blue and the sunlight was pouring all over the sports fields. The colours were bright, the temperature had bounced and deodorants were suddenly essential. Girls lay in clumps on the grass. Boys charged about and wrestled with each other. Some of them had started a football game. The morning break was so short you wouldn't have thought it was worth it, but they always did it if they could. They could go from bell to ball to rolling in the mud in three minutes flat. Tough luck on whoever would be sitting next to them in third period.

Sally wanted to be out there too. It was the next thing on her list for the day. Shakespeare essay – ✓, done that. Hand it in – ✓, done that. Spend break in sun – ✓ . . . Hey, what's the hold-up? Can't he mark it sometime else?

(And why's he squiggling? It should have been *²⁰⁄₂₀ Very Good*. Easy.)

Five minutes of break had gone already.

Another five and she'd have just time to say 'Hi' to her group before they all had to come back in again. *'How was your summer?' 'Yeah, great, thanks – I spent the whole of it with Mr Kingsley, getting my English marked.'* (Sarcastic cheers.)

Alec Gardner was out there, and so were Tony Hicks and Zac Stenton – the three gods of Year Twelve. All of them were lean-faced, lean-bodied and had some secret way of never getting any spots. Alec's hair was blond and curly. His teeth were white and he smiled a lot. Tony was brown-haired and brown-skinned and had been voted the most perfect tan in the school. Zac was taller, dark, and he actually did notice you from time to time. Sally thought he was nice.

She wasn't especially thinking about any of them. That was just where her eyes went. Same as everyone else's did.

She was thinking about how to save the world. Weather like this was OK, but it also reminded her that global warming was on its way. Monsoons were coming to Darlington. So were all the poor people from the lands around the Mediterranean which would have turned to desert. Everybody said it and nobody seemed to be doing very much about it. So Sally had added 'Stop Global Warming' to her list. And stop it she would. She just needed to get enough people to see what had to be done.

She was also wondering if she would get Mr Kingsley for English next year. Mr Kingsley was quite mad in at least three different ways. Six terms times three different madnesses equalled eighteen terms of chronic insanity. She didn't think she could cope.

But then pretty well all the teachers at Darlington High were mad one way or another. For her GCSE options for next year she was going to have to choose between taking Music with Mr Bright, Drama with Mrs Popham or (shudder) P.E. with Miss Tackle. Mr Bright and Mrs Popham and Miss Tackle were all just as mad as Mr Kingsley. Rumour had it that Miss Tackle had changed her name by deed poll.

Mr Kingsley's sorts of madness were: i) being about thirty but looking sixty; ii) being pale and grey and long-nosed and sitting so slumped in his seat that his back curved like a snail's shell; and iii) dreaming about the love life he had never had. He also mumbled poetry.

'Hm,' said Mr Kingsley, and squiggled again.

Twelve minutes left of break.

And she was thinking about Viola Matson. She was wondering if Viola really was getting some-where with Tony. Cassie, Viola and all that group always acted as if they were older and more sophisticated than the other Year Nines. They hung about looking haughty and they went to parties with the sixth-formers (sometimes they were even invited). And word had just come round the Year Nine girls that if anyone *else* were seen near Tony, that person would live only long enough to regret her mistake very much indeed. Signed, Viola and co. You didn't usually get one of those unless something was going on.

But hey, nobody could stop you looking.

'"I, being poor, have only my dreams,"' sighed Mr Kingsley (in relation to nothing at all, as far as Sally could tell).

Eleven minutes. Maybe she would have time to walk out there and at least reach her group before they all came back in again. Maybe she would get to say 'hey' to Zac or Alec as she passed.

Maybe she could dye her hair white and make her eyes up in black and undo her top button and yank her tie-knot halfway down her chest and wear a skirt that covered just the top two centimetres of her thigh. And if she did, maybe people like Zac and Alec and Tony would look at her a bit more. If she could somehow possibly do all that and still be for real.

She was not thinking about the birthday.

The birthday was on Sunday.

She was Not Thinking About It.

'Not bad at all,' said Mr Kingsley at last. 'Apart from the introduction.'

'What's wrong with my introduction?'

Mr Kingsley cleared his throat. '"Love, present in every Shakespearian comedy,"' he read from Sally's page, '". . . is a theme accessible to all: young and old, rich and poor, man and woman. *Midsummer Night's Dream* is not to be found lacking . . ." (indeed it is not). ". . . The first, rather unfortunately warty, example of love I am going to explore is that between Helena and Demetrius . . ."'

He stopped, pushed his varifocals to the end of his nose and peered sadly at her over the top of them. The whites of his eyes had a whingey tinge of grey in them as if they had gone a little bit mouldy.

'"Rather unfortunately warty?"' he murmured.

'She loves him. He's dumped her. So she tells him the girl he wants has run off to the woods to escape him. That's just stupid. And she knows he's no good. She says so.'

'She does indeed.' Mr Kingsley returned his varifocals to the 'close' position. He squinted at the paper.

'Things base and vile, holding no quantity,
Love can transpose to form and dignity.
Love looks not with the eyes, but with the mind.
And therefore is wing'd Cupid painted blind.'

'This, in your view, is "warty"?'

'It's putrid. She knows what he is, but she chases after him anyway.'

'The greatest English poet is saying that Love transforms things into something better.'

'I think the greatest poet just meant us to laugh at her.'

Mr Kingsley looked glum. He lived a lonely life, but in his heart he clung to the belief that one day some model or film starlet would see him from afar, fall for him madly and carry him away to unending True Love. He clung to it, and at the same time lived in quiet terror that the World would find out his belief and laugh at him cruelly.

Sadly for Mr Kingsley, the World could read him like a book. This was because he mumbled love poems to himself and sighed aloud over pictures of models and film starlets. It rather gave him away.

It was also clear to everyone – including all his Year Eight, Nine, Ten and GCSE pupils – that Mr

Kingsley actually knew as much about True Love as a frog knew about gourmet cooking, i.e. he had next to no chance of experiencing it and, if he ever did, it would be painful, surprising and very horribly fatal to his existence. Sally was quite worried for him sometimes.

'"I swear to thee, by Cupid's strongest bow / By his best arrow with the golden head" . . . This does not appeal? No? Very well. I will allow any view, so long as you are able to support it with argument. A shame that we are not studying Austen this year. You would enjoy *Sense and Sensibility*.'

'I've read it.'

'And?'

'I liked the "Sense" bit.'

'I see. Perhaps we should try a different theme.' Mr Kingsley rummaged in his briefcase. 'Something to keep you occupied while the others are finishing theirs.'

Sally hesitated. Then she shrugged. 'Sure,' she said.

'Explore that idea of yours, hm? Laughter in Shakespeare. Interesting one. You might look at this . . . '

He dragged out a dog-eared old exam paper that was the colour of dried cream. The text was marked with many underlinings and words were pencilled illegibly in the margins. He marked a question with a cross and handed it to her. '. . . You'll need to read your way into a tragedy or two. It's a pity we don't start *Othello* until next term. But you'll some useful stuff in chapter eight of the textbook. I'm sure you'll cope.'

'Oh. Thanks.'

So that was: 1) read next term's Shakespeare as well as this one; 2) read a minimum of one more that they weren't going to do at all this year; 3) write essay that no one else was being asked to write. Grimly Sally added them all to her list. She wasn't going to leave them not done if they were there to be done. But right now they ranked well below Tony Hicks and Global Warming and dress sense in the order of priority.

The question on the paper read 'Comedy and Tragedy: how thin is Shakespeare's line between laughter and tears?'

'Happy Birthday,' she muttered.

Mr Kingsley's sparse eyebrows furrowed upwards.

'Sorry,' said Sally. 'I've got birthdays on the brain.'

'Yours?'

'It's at the weekend.'

'Congratulations.' He began to gather up his books

and papers (of which there were many). After a little while he realized that Sally was still in the room.

'Are you waiting for me?' he said.

Sally shook her head. 'I'm in here next period,' she said. 'Might as well just stay.'

'Very good.'

The classroom door closed behind him. Outside, a football rose high into the air, fell and was caught by brown, long-fingered hands. Sally heard Tony whoop. She saw Zac Stenton grinning. Who was going to be sitting with those guys next period?

Her next period was French. Of course she didn't have her French books with her. She'd have to go round to her locker and fetch them back here. She might as well do that now. Except that what she wanted to do was stop here and look out of the window.

(Cupid? Stupid!)

Punt, whoop, laughter. A plane trailed its white wake across the sky. More carbon in the atmosphere. How long could this last?

Not thinking about the birthday.

Clangaclangaclangaclangaclangaclangaclangaclang! The bell. The sounds of feet on stairs. Voices calling. Suddenly everyone outside was on their feet and drifting in towards the building. Her French books were still in her locker on the far side of the quad. She had to go and get them. It would be just dumb to be late, after spending the whole of morning break in the place she was supposed to be. People were already crowding along the corridors, books in their arms and bags over their shoulders. Sally crowded with them, looking vaguely around for Alec and Tony and Zac but not really expecting to see them.

Then, suddenly, the crowds *were* Alec and Tony and Zac, tall and white-shirted, shouldering towards her from the other direction. Alec still had the ball under his arm. Sally's jaw had just time to drop. Her mouth had just time to say 'Hey.' Alec passed her and he hadn't heard.

Tony had. He said 'Hey-Hey,' back. Though Sally wasn't sure he knew who had spoken to him.

'Hey, Sally,' said Zac. He smiled. 'How's your summer?'

'Mr Kingsley . . . English . . .' said Sally.

That was all there was time for. Even the roll of her eyes had to be done over her shoulder. The crowds closed in again. She pushed on towards her locker, towards the books, the lists, the ✓s that were jostling for their place in her day.

3: DOUBLE EVIL

A voice spoke in her mind. It said:

'Why not ask them?'

'Tony etc? To the birthday? Because I don't want to get laughed at by the entire school, that's why. Plus I'd get murdered by Viola.'

'Ah. But I've got you thinking about birthdays now, haven't I?'

Sally's body was moving down a school corridor at a brisk walk. In her mind, she was also in the corridor. But now a whiteboard had appeared ahead of her and was preceding her down it at the same pace as she was walking. Standing at the whiteboard, wielding a marker, was a small (and warty) little person with beady eyes, flabby grey skin and a red pillbox hat.

From under the hat peeped tufts of gingery hair, and also two tiny horns. His name was Muddlespot.

Swiftly Muddlespot sketched on his travelling whiteboard a picture of Sally and her twin sister Billie. It was obvious which girl he meant to be Billie because he drew her with a massive frown and a mouth that was open to say something really loud and unpleasant. Grinning, he added a banner that read 'HAPY BIRTDAY'.

'Two birthdays for the price of one,' he smirked. 'So nice to have a twin! What could be better?'

'I know where you're going with this,' said Sally.

Muddlespot's grin widened. 'Shall we just remember all the birthdays we can?'

'All right,' Sally groaned. 'Bring it on.'

There was a pattern to birthdays in Sally's house. Each one was different. But every year things were somehow the same.

SCENES FROM
BIRTHDAYS PAST

Scene 1

BILLIE (aged 4):   It's not FAIR!

MUM: (patiently) Sweetheart – yours has got *lovely* fur! Feel it. Isn't it nice . . . ?

BILLIE: I wanted a *BIG* Teddy!!!

MUM: They're *almost* the same size, look. Let's measure them back to back. Stand up, Teddies, nice and straight . . .'

BILLIE: **AOWWOAWOAWOAWWW!!!!!**

SALLY (aged 4):   We can swap Teddies. I don't mind.

MUM: Oh, sweetheart . . . are you sure . . . ?

Scene 5 *(this was a long one)*

BILLIE (aged 8):   It's not FAIR!

MUM: (baffled) But sweetheart – they're exactly the same! You can count the beads . . .

BILLIE: But hers is PINK!!!

Scene 9

BILLIE (aged 12): It's not FAIR!

MUM: (desperate) Sweetheart – you've already *got* a mobile . . . !

BILLIE: But hers is *fourth* generation!!

MUM: Is it?

SALLY (aged 12): Here. Let's save time . . .

MUM: Oh, *Sally*!

BILLIE: Cheers. *(beep)*

SALLY: . . . I could probably use another radio alarm, anyway.

BILLIE: *(beep)*

MUM: (sighing) OK – is everyone happy now?

BILLIE: 'Think so. *(beep)* How do you switch this off?

SALLY: Try using a hammer.

It was coming. Sometime in the next few days there was going to be an earthquake of a row. Everyone at home knew it. Sally knew it, Billie knew it, Mum knew it. Greg (Mum's current partner) knew it. Shades the cat had moved into his bomb shelter behind the umbrella stand.

It was like a storm on the horizon, like the GCSEs next year. You could feel it the moment you stepped through the door. The house was chaos. Mum was beside herself. The toaster wasn't working and Greg was keeping his nose glued to a magazine or a computer or TV screen, which was driving Mum doubly beside herself. All this was as it always was. But there was something beneath it all: a feeling as if everything in No. 19 Darlington Row – every object, every person, everything down to the spiders in the crevices and the house mites in the dust – was slowly winding itself taut.

A week before the birthday, even the tea started tasting different.

'. . . I *am* listening,' said Sally (in her mind, as her hands worked automatically to dig her French books out of her locker). 'But you're not making sense.'

'Sense?' said Muddlespot in injured tones. 'How much more sense do you want?'

'You said Billie thinks I'm stupid because she can get anything she wants just by shouting for it.'

'Yes.'

'But just now you said she shouts because *she*

feels stupid and she thinks I'm the one who has everything.'

'I said that?' Muddlespot tried to look innocent. For someone like him, this was actually quite difficult.

'Several times.'

'I am what I am,' said Muddlespot, giving up on looking innocent and trying instead to look superior. 'I don't *have* to be consistent. Nowhere in my job description does it say—'

'I'll notice if you're not. Now get on with it. You're in charge of this class, aren't you?'

There was a quick flurry in Sally's mind. On the board the banner now read HAP^{p}Y BIRT^{h}DAY and the two girls looked a lot more like Sally and Billie than they had at first. That was because Sally had come up, taken the marker and redrawn them. She had also corrected Muddlespot's spelling. She had even added (with what he felt was a touch of unnecessary sarcasm) a school timetable, and had labelled the current period 'Double Evil'.

You're in charge of this class, aren't you? Sure, sure . . .

There was only one person in charge here. It wasn't him.

'So,' he said, feeling a bit shaken and in need of

a holiday in the heart of some volcano. 'So, where were we? Here we have the presents Billie is going to get' – he drew a large pile of blocks in front of the picture of Billie – 'and here's what you'll get . . .' He drew a single very small square in front of Sally.

'Mum's not that stupid,' said Sally. 'If she did that Billie would have a row with her about not being fair on *me*.'

'Er – would she?'

'It's more complicated than you think. Here. While you've been talking I've written an essay. You've got to mark it.'

Muddlespot looked at the twenty closely-written pages she handed him. It was titled *Why Should I be Bothered about Birthdays?* He felt stunned.

'. . . I included some reasons you don't seem to have thought of,' said Sally.

'Oh,' said Muddlespot.

'. . . On both sides . . .'

'I suppose you have,' said Muddlespot sourly.

'. . . And you have to set me some homework,' said Sally. 'All my teachers do.'

'Ah, yes,' said Muddlespot 'Um. Think of three things you want on your birthday that no one's going to give you.'

29

'Easy,' said Sally. 'A sunny day, world peace and an end to poverty.'

Muddlespot wondered how many of Sally's teachers shot themselves.

'If you don't mind,' he said, 'I think I need to lie down.'

'Then perhaps it is my turn,' said another voice.

A powerful figure stepped forward. He was winged, dressed in a neat white dinner jacket and wore a purple bow tie. His jaw was strong and square. His forehead was high and square. Under his crisp white shirt his muscles were massive – and square. His wings were of white light (and they were square too). His flaming eyes were shaded behind Raybans of translucent ebony. He was an angel, but no ordinary angel. He was the closest the heavenly hosts came to a decorated hero.

His name was Windleberry.

Confronted by Evil, Windleberry knew what to do. He smote. And when Evil had been properly smitten he chased it howling back into the dark, hot places from which it had come. In his experience, this worked every time. It would have worked now. He out-numbered poor Muddlespot ten to one all by himself.

But he was here to be Sally's guardian angel, and for Guardians the rules were a bit different. A

Guardian was supposed to be an idea in the mind he was guarding. Muddlespot, too, was an idea, albeit a vile and loathsome one inserted by The Enemy. Ideas couldn't just start smiting each other. It caused confusion and headaches and things. What happened when two opposing ideas met in a human mind depended very much on the mind's owner, and the rules they set.

Quite a lot of minds said straight away that they didn't want any Guardians or Enemies, thank you. Too much like hard work. So both Guardian and Enemy got taken off and locked up in the very deepest darkest dungeons that the mind had, along with all the other ideas that the mind didn't want to think about. *Then* both Guardian and Enemy would have to escape – there was usually a way – and hide themselves in corners, watching for a chance to speak, and when they came out they had to disguise themselves as something other than they really were so they didn't just get thrown in jail again.

Sally's mind was fundamentally more organized than this. She knew Windleberry, and she knew Muddlespot. Fair enough. If they thought they had something to say, she made them stand up and say it. And then Sally got to say what she was going to do.

This was how Good and Evil and Free Will all managed to be in the same place together at the same time.

Windleberry strode to the whiteboard and grasped the board rubber as if it were a lance of fire. He frowned upon the things Muddlespot had drawn there. He put up his hand to wipe the slate clean. Then he thought, Use the Lie of The Enemy against him. Yay verily, let it be.

'There was a Mother who had Three Daughters,' he intoned, rapidly expanding Muddlespot's drawing with neat and quick strokes of his own. 'To the one she gave Ten Presents. To the second she gave Five Presents. And to the third she gave but One. And she said unto them, "Play with these for the day, while I am at my office. And when I return, tell me what you have done . . ."'

'Let me give you a clue here,' said Sally. 'We're not babies any more. This won't be about presents. It'll be about who gets invited, I bet you. How many of her friends can come. That kind of thing.'

Windleberry hesitated, for about a sixteenth of a second.

Once again he was drawing on the board. 'There was a Girl who was throwing a Party. And she said unto her Mother, "Go out and invite all my friends to come to my Party." And Her Mother did go. But her friends began to make excuses. One said "I have just bought a new pony and I must go and see it . . .""

Windleberry was in his element. Standing up and declaring The Truth came naturally to him. (He had an advantage over Muddlespot here.) He never doubted himself. He never got discouraged. For him, defeat was a learning experience, disaster just a step on the road to victory. He was perfect in everything he did. He could split a mountain with a thunderbolt or tune a snowflake until it was exactly the right shade of blue. He could count the leaves on a tree and the spines on a hedgehog's back. His sermons could make a galaxy swear off the ammonia for the rest of its fifteen billion years of existence. His handwriting was both neat and absolutely clear. He also played the tenor sax.

He had served in a hundred different departments in Heaven and had made his mark in each one. He never questioned his orders. He never complained how difficult it was. When he was given a job, he did it until it was done. If he had a fault, it was that he could sometimes be just a little bit too perfect. This is quite hard to achieve in Heaven. But . . .

Just a moment ago, Mr Kingsley had used the word 'cupid'. He had done it twice, as if he actually knew what a cupid was. He didn't know half so well as Windleberry.

Windleberry had been a cupid himself, a long time ago.

Cupids are a peculiar sort of angel. They shoot golden arrows at people and make them fall in love, after which lots of exciting things happen. They have their own special dress code and way of speaking, and they also have a subversive tendency to attach little hearts of pink card to their arrows, bearing messages along the lines of 'You have been served by . . .'

But only one cupid *ever* has attached a note to his arrow that began: 'If you are not completely satisfied with our service . . .' and went on to outline, in detail and over fifty pages of tightly written script, the exact and correct procedure for bringing a complaint against Heaven itself.

Fifty pages. It was a wonder the arrow hit its target at all. But then it was Windleberry who fired it.

There had been a bit of trouble about that at the time. Some members of the Celestial Staff Room felt that Heaven was, by definition, Heaven, that all the actions of Heaven were determined by the Great Curriculum, and that there could never possibly be anything for anyone to complain about.

Others had said it just proved that the Great Curriculum was due for an overhaul, since there were parts of it that one or two colleagues – mentioning no names – clearly didn't understand.

And the Department of Love, to which all cupids belong, refused to take responsibility for any of it, because being sensible and responsible and fair-minded and worrying about customer satisfaction etc was absolutely the opposite of what Love was supposed to be about.

The discussion got unusually heated. Pews got ripped up, cassocks got pulled down and the crowd spilled out onto the sports pitches. A record number of yellow cards got shown by the Celestial Referee.

That was a very long time ago. No trace of the cupid remained in the lean figure who spoke in Sally's mind.

But the thing about Heaven is, it does go on for ever.

Some people do remember it all.

4: THE APPEALS BOARD

It's true, by the way. Heaven is a school. Or something very like one.

It's supposed to be a secret, just in case anyone on Earth thinks that being stuck at the back of a class for all Eternity is *not* their idea of Heaven and they won't bother to apply. But when you look at it, it has to be true.

There's a Head. The Head of Everything, in fact, though he doesn't often come out of his study.

There's also the Governors. Exactly who gets to be a Governor, and what they do when they are one, is a bit of a mystery. Just like a school.

There are all those big, powerful archangels and seraphs and things, who've been around for thousands and thousands of years. They're the teachers. OK, so they've got six pairs of wings each and several thousand eyes and flaming swords, but *all the same* they're just like teachers. They go into meetings together and then they come out and stride around carrying scrolls and looking important. You don't get to be cheeky to their faces. And be careful what you do when they've passed on down the corridor too. Some of those eyes are on the backs of their heads. Just like teachers have.

There are all the human souls who come in through the gates. Hundreds of thousands arrive every day, wide-eyed, wandering around looking lost and just asking to have their lunch money beaten out of them, if that sort of thing ever happened in Heaven (it doesn't). These are the pupils, of course.

There are rules, which in Heaven are called 'Laws' or 'Commandments'. There are libraries. There are choirs. There are also clubs, debating societies, arts and drama etc. There are even some sports pitches. But above all, there are classes.

Ah yes, the classes. That's because . . .

Humans have this idea that at the end of their lives they're going to wake up perfect and knowing everything. It's just not like that. There are *so* many things they still have to learn. Ask any angel you like, it'll tell you it's true. That's what the classes are for.

And what Eternity is for. Isn't that a comforting thought?

OK, so Heaven has a few things most schools don't have, like Thrones and Crystal Seas and a bunch of uniformed Celestial Inspection Angels (who will come in later) and also a Department of Geography that spends half its time planning to end the world. So as schools go, it's pretty unusual. Plus, it lasts for ever and is big enough to house everyone who has ever lived.

Or about half of them, anyway.

It's also the school that everyone wants to get into. Because, whatever you think about sitting in the back of a class for all Eternity, there isn't a lot of choice. Once you've seen the Other Place, you do want to go to Heaven. You really, really do.

The way you get in is you sit an exam. It's long and complicated, and it takes the whole of your life to complete. You get handed your results at the end of it. There's a pass mark. If you've made it, great. If not, bad luck. Very Bad Luck. It was nice knowing you.

And there's an Appeals Board. If you haven't got in and you think you should have done, you can go to Appeal, just like when you're trying to get into a school that's over-subscribed. Heaven takes its appeals very seriously. It spends a lot of time on each one. Time is something Heaven has lots of.

This means that if you do go to Appeal, you'd better be prepared for a wait. There are folks in the queue ahead of you who've been waiting for . . .

'Three *thousand* years?' cried Mishamh.

'There's a bit of a backlog,' admitted Doomsday. 'One rather difficult case has been holding things up. When they've sorted it out everything should move more quickly.'

'*One* case that's been going on for three *thousand* years?'

They flew together through the great Gallery of Penitence. The dark angel was like a thundercloud and his assistant like a white dove caught in a sunbeam beside him. The floor of the Gallery was thronged with souls: standing, sitting, patiently shifting from foot to foot, squatting in tents or playing endless games of cards or dice (which are generally frowned on in Heaven but are allowed in the Appeals Queue as a way of saying 'Sorry about the Delay'). The Gallery of Penitence ended in the Stair of Sincerity, which has ten thousand steps, each the size of a football pitch. The crowd filled every inch of them. It carpeted the floor of the Hall of Lamentation, which is the length of a comet's tail, and it zigzagged around the vast, eight-sided Lobby of the Law until it ended finally at the great dark door over which was written in letters the colour of sunset:

BOARD OF APPEALS
PLEASE WAIT TO BE CALLED

The doors were of black pearl and the handles were carved from the sound of a great brass gong. Hung upon one of the handles was another sign.

APPEAL IN PROGRESS
QUIET PLEASE

The souls nearest the door looked up as Doomsday approached. They looked a bit tired and worn, as well they might after having to wait in silence for three thousand years. They bowed respectfully to Doomsday and he bowed back. He had passed them many times before. Ignoring the door handles (which would let off gong-noises if anyone touched them, of course) he placed his palm on the door of black pearl and pushed. It swung silently inwards, revealing a short passage that opened at the far end into a huge space. On one side of the passage was a small opening. Doomsday ducked through it and led Mishamh up a long flight of narrow stairs, to emerge at last on a high gallery that swept all the way around a huge room like the upper circle in an opera house that had been built for giants.

Directly opposite Mishamh, against the far wall, were three mountain-high statues that rose from floor to ceiling. One was of white marble, one was of red sandstone, one was of grey granite. Their faces were huge and passionless, like the Sphinx of Egypt. Their carved wings were folded around their shoulders and down their sides. Their chests were muscular and bare. And on their foreheads were carved the words MERCY, JUSTICE and (more worryingly) VENGEANCE.

At their waists the carvings ended. They became smooth blocks like pillars that fell all the way to the floor. It was as if the heavenly sculptors had got that far and then given up in exhaustion, thinking, That's enough. Anyone who sees them will get the idea. Anyway – why would they want legs? *These* guys aren't going anywhere.

They were not. They never had been. They would

carry on standing there until the end (whenever that might be). They were in no hurry. They looked down on the soul before them with the same appraising, unchanging stare. They had not blinked once in three thousand years.

The soul was a woman. She stood alone in the centre of that vast chamber. She was tall, handsome and dressed in a plain white robe of the sort worn by a civilization that had collapsed thousands of years ago. Her hair was dark and done in ringlets. Her skin was lightly tanned. She wore no jewellery, because no one does in Heaven.

Before her, on a table made of pure, polished rose-petal, lay a golden arrow. Attached to the arrow was a thick roll of parchment. Even in Heaven, where nothing ever gets old, the parchment had gone a bit yellow and curly and looked as if it had lain exactly where it was for rather a long time. Seated high up in the galleries, Mishamh, with his angel's eyes, could make out the first line easily. In handwriting that was both neat and absolutely clear, it read:

'If you are not completely satisfied with our service ...'

Beyond the woman there was a strange and forbidding hole in the floor. It took up nearly one third of the central area. Mishamh could not see down into the bottom. It just dropped into blackness. He wondered if it even had a bottom, or if, supposing he happened to fall in there, he would just fall for ever. (Angels do not like the thought of falling. An angel who Falls is generally Bad News, so anything to do with falling is pretty much a sore point.)

Two more figures stood on either side of the woman. The nearer one was another angel, who was at that moment addressing the Board. But the other was grey-skinned and red-eyed, with . . . yes . . . *horns*.

An extraordinary, crawling feeling came over Mishamh. He could not quite believe what he was seeing.

Here? How was it possible?

Could it really be what he thought it was? Surely it should be – well, cackling, salivating, dancing wildly and making rude gestures with its fingers?

Its very stillness disturbed him. Its eyes were half closed. It too looked as if it had been where it was for a very long time.

'Sir . . .' he whispered. 'Is that . . .'

'It is The Enemy. One of them.'

Mishamh shuddered. 'Why . . . that is, I mean – nobody's smiting it!'

'It has immunity. It is here as a witness. It is also here so that if the Board says "Take Her Down", the taking down can be done with suitable effect.'

Mishamh looked at the hole in the floor and shuddered. 'But – it's disgusting! We'll be gratifying its cruel lusts! We'll be pandering to . . .'

'Quite.'

'Can't we do anything?'

'We can have Patience, Mishamh. The Enemy has lived with this soul all her life, just as our Guardian colleague there has. Its evidence is a necessary part of the Appeal. You must remember that.'

'Yes, sir,' said the angel obediently.

'However. If you *should* happen to catch it in the corridors . . .'

'Sir?'

'Then you may jostle it a bit.'

Mishamh looked glumly at the horned figure. He doubted that it would be unwise enough to step even an inch outside the courts. But if it did, then yes, there would be a jostle. *Quite* a jostle.

He was planning a hundred-metre run-up, for a start.

Because The Enemy were working against the Great Curriculum! They spread Ignorance. They spread Fear! They met the fresh, bright-eyed souls on the path to Heaven and said: 'You don't want to go there. That place is only for posh kids. Come behind the bike sheds and see what we've got.'

Creation was infested with them. Because of their evil influence barely half of all human souls made the pass mark in the Entrance Exam. There was no getting rid of them. As long as the world existed they would be there to twist the truths of Heaven and make them a trap for the unwary.

And that was why the world had to end. It was obvious. The purpose of Heaven was to make things perfect. The Earth could not be perfect. Therefore the Earth must be destroyed. It was the only way, now, that the Great Curriculum could be rescued. Man must be set free, to enter Heaven at last amid general rejoicing. Then all the unpleasant subjects like Sorrow and Greed and Death could be dropped and everyone could settle down to studying the real stuff for all the rest of Eternity. Mishamh was quite looking forward to having a small tutorial group of, say, ten thousand souls or so, with whom he would spend the next few million years on the subject of Wonder, explaining all the marvellous things in the physical universe that they had so sadly missed during their time down below.

But before then there was a rescue to perform. Fates had decreed that he, Mishamh, would be the liberator. He clasped the file marked

```
┌────────────────────────────────────────────┐
│  ASTEROID (38562975) Zebukun                 │
└────────────────────────────────────────────┘
```

more closely under his arm. It nestled there, fierce and firm, like the hilt of a fiery sword.

One of the statues spoke. It had a high, cold voice, but because its lips did not move it was hard to tell which of the statues it was. By turning his head and moving his position a bit Mishamh worked out that it must be the one of marble, marked MERCY. Mercy was questioning a witness.

At length. Using a lot of long words.

In fact it wasn't really asking questions at all. It was more sort of . . .

'. . . the proposition that your Department *knowingly* and *materially* interfered in this candidate's examination, causing the suspension of Free Will, and her subjection at the very least to Desires, and arguably to Influences that could be said to represent *Divine Intervention*, whereupon the answers she entered to questions 2304(a) through to 6823(d) part iii upon the examination paper concerning Adultery, Illegal Marriage, War and Destruction were materially affected, implying that the *responsibility* for the answers submitted rest properly with your Department and not with the candidate . . .'

When it fell silent, which happened some time later, it did so with an air of satisfaction. And although not one of the stone faces changed in the slightest, there was a perceptible brightening of the atmosphere, as if the three great presences were somehow pleased by the way the question had been asked. Which they were. In their book, using no fewer than three thousand seven hundred and thirty-two words to say 'Come on, admit it – it was all your fault, wasn't it?' was an achievement worth celebrating.

The speech had been addressed to the witness box, where the witness was situated. This was a cupid.

It is not difficult to recognize a cupid. For a start, they are shorter than anyone else in Heaven. The cupid was not only standing *in* a box; he was very probably standing *on* one.

And cupids are always stark naked. No one knows why, but they are. It's not as if their bodies are anything to boast about. Their cheeks are fat, their bellies are round, they have at least two chins each and their little willies hang down like points between their flabby thighs. In Heaven, which has a fairly strict School Uniform Policy, meeting a cupid can be a shock. The first reaction is almost always to avert your eyes. (The second is to wonder, since cupids are after all a sort of angel, what they could possibly be using those little things *for*.)

'WOZZN'T US,' said the cupid. Its voice was startlingly deep. 'WOZ SOME GUY 'OO'S LEFT.'

There was a moment's pause. Even after millennia of dealing with cupids, the Appeals Board couldn't help feeling that there should have been more than this.

'Wait a moment,' said the red sandstone statue (JUSTICE), in a voice as dry as desert wind. 'Wait. We've been here before . . .'

'We've been here before at least twenty times,' said the grey granite (VENGEANCE), and its voice was like a landslide that buries a city.

'. . . and what we *said*,' said the red sandstone, determined not to be interrupted, 'was that we should consider all acts performed by the nominally separate persons of cupids, cherubs, winged messengers and the specific manifestations known variously as Venus, Aphrodite, Aidin, Branwen, Chalchiuhtlicue, Erzulie, Hathor et cetera et cetera, to rest *in substance* within the *Department of The Angel of Love*. Are we to understand that the Department now wishes to submit further arguments for consideration on this point?'

'Wozzn't us,' said the cupid again.

A sigh rustled around the nearly empty chamber. The woman bowed her head. She shifted her weight slightly to the other foot.

'We shall naturally entertain any *new* arguments the Department is pleased to put forward,' said the sandstone. 'The mere assertion that the Department of Love was not responsible, however . . .'

'What did she do?' whispered Mishamh.

'She fell in love with a man,' said Doomsday, 'and left her husband for him. There was a war and a city was destroyed.'

'She destroyed a city?'

'I believe that was question ten thousand and something,' said Doomsday. 'The Board is still looking at her answers to questions two thousand to seven thousand, which are mainly about whether it was her fault that she fell in love. It's a test case. A lot of other appeals you saw waiting outside will depend upon what's decided here.'

Mishamh thought about this.

'When you say "a lot" . . .'

The dead are not numberless. Not to an angel. They've set up a counter on the wall just inside the Pearly Gates to keep an exact total. But it's quite hard to get a reading because the last dial is a bit of a blur.

'. . . Don't they *all* fall in love?'

'Most of them do. At least, they say so.'

'But . . . but . . . shouldn't they hurry this up? There's a deadline from the Governors!'

'I'm afraid,' said Doomsday slowly, 'that the Governors will put back the deadline to allow time for the appeal. That's what they've always done in the past.'

Asteroid (38562975) Zebukun. Six months to impact. If the deadline was put back, Zebukun would not happen. Nothing would come of all the work and thought he had devoted to it. Nothing, except that his plan would be shelved . . .

In the Library.

It would be placed in the huge Library of

Geography, where the bookcases were already stuffed with plans for the end of the world, all of which had been dutifully written to meet the Governors' deadlines. And which had been postponed, one after another, because . . .

Now Mishamh understood the meaning of that library. He understood why none of those plans had ever happened. A pit seemed to open in his stomach, as deep and dark as the one in the floor.

'But they *can't*! There's the Curriculum . . . !'

The file pressed beneath Mishamh's arm: solid, meticulous, beautiful – and betrayed.

'Can't they just get it decided?' he cried, desperately.

'B♥gger ♥ff!' said the cupid.

A delicate shudder ran around the Court. The Board was (momentarily) lost for words. The marble column turned a shade of pink. Then VENGEANCE spoke.

'The remark of the witness contravenes the Rule laid down in Governors' Memo No. 88463 "Re: Conduct of Appeals Board Business," it grated, in tones like a slide of shale.

'♥♥♥♥ all of you!' said the cupid.

'This is *unacceptable*. The witness will stand

51

down until further notice. We wish to discuss his conduct with the Angel of Love.'

'Love, you see, comes from Heaven,' said Doomsday, as he left the chamber with his assistant trailing sadly alongside him. 'It is itself a part of the Great Curriculum. Suppose, then, that a woman falls in love, and because of her love a city is destroyed and she fails her examination. Should she be handed over to The Enemy for that reason?'

'No, sir. Not if the Department of Love made it happen.'

Doomsday's mouth twitched into a wry smile. 'I see that you will never be a philosopher, Mishamh. You have made your argument in just eleven words.'

'Thank you, sir.'

'Alas, the Board does not find it so simple. They have got themselves into something of a loop. Every fifty years or so they come around to the same point and start arguing it out all over again. It's because Love is involved, you see. She has no intention of taking responsibility for wars or tragedies or anything. It makes it very difficult for the Board to get a handle on things. Frankly, Love is running rings around them.'

'But the Appeals Board should overrule her!'

'The Appeals Board,' mused Doomsday, 'are very professional colleagues. I have the highest regard for their work. So, unfortunately, have they.'

Mishamh was silent.

'Well,' said Doomsday gently. 'This asteroid of yours. Any chance we could, ah, ask it to call back later?'

When the young angel spoke, his voice was hoarse. 'In about two thousand six hundred years, sir. It's got quite a long orbit.'

'I see. I'm sorry.'

The aide rallied bravely. 'We could do something with sunspots, sir.'

'Sunspots?'

'Affecting radio transmissions. Particle bombardment, aircraft fall out of sky, computer failure, reorder systems affected, panic buying, starvation – that sort of thing?'

'Hm. Weren't you going to do an alien invasion?'

'They're still travelling. About another million years to go.'

'A million? *Long*-term planning, I see.'

'That's all we could do with that one, sir. We're looking at dropping the invasion fleet into a black hole, but . . .'

'No. Try the sunspots. I like the sunspots. Will they take long?'

'We'll need several cycles, sir.'

'Do your best,' said Doomsday.

Do your best, thought Mishamh. To meet the next deadline that would come down from the Governors. Which would then be postponed, like all the other deadlines before it. So yet more souls would be born, and fall in love. So that there would be even more cases queuing on the Stair of Sincerity. And yet more deadlines would be postponed . . .

In his arms he cradled the Zebukun folder as if it were a dying child. His throat was burning and there was a stinging sensation in his eyes. He was badly in need of some fire-retardant tissues.

'This shouldn't be *happening*!'

Among angels, Innocence is highly prized. Doomsday wished he had some of it himself.

'I have said so to the Governors. The Governors have written memos to the Appeals Board. And the Appeals Board has said that everything will be sorted out once it's all been duly weighed and pondered and considered and the witnesses from the Department of Love have provided a full explanation of their position and so forth.'

'But – the Governors *set* the Great Curriculum!' Mishamh cried. 'The Great Curriculum says the world has to end! Nothing makes sense if it doesn't! Wh—'

Just in time, he caught Doomsday's warning look. Just in time, he bit down with his own celestial teeth upon his own angelic tongue. It hurt. But that was all right, because pain and suffering were part of the Great Curriculum too. For the time being.

What was *not* part of the Curriculum was the use of the word he had nearly uttered – that word 'Why?' In Heaven, there was no 'Why?' If a thing was, then it was as it should be.

'Ah, yes,' said Doomsday.

'Er . . . yes, sir?'

'Yes. I have a theory about this.'

But that was all he said.

Mishamh scuttled beside him, trying to keep pace. He almost bumped into two figures who emerged from a passage that led to the back of the witness box. They were cupids. Scowling, Mishamh averted his eyes. He hurried on after his master.

'Nice one,' said one cupid to the other.

'Yeah,' said the second cupid, who was the one that had been in the witness box. His name was Fug.

'Give 'em the finger,' said his fellow.

'Ev'ry time,' said Fug.

They flew off down the corridor to tell their boss she was in trouble again. That's 'flew' as in 'propelled themselves with their wings without their feet having to touch the ground'. Other angels soar and swoop and stoop like eagles from Heaven. But a cupid in flight is more like a drunken bumblebee. They are not very aerodynamic.

The fact is that some of Heaven's rules do apply to cupids. They are different from the rules that other angels have to follow, but they're still rules and the cupids have to stick by them. They set out, among other things, exactly what a cupid is allowed to wear, i.e. nothing. They say exactly how fat each cheek must be, that one chin (but not both) must have a dimple in it, the size of each roll of flesh that must be worn, and of course the fact that nothing must be worn on top of that. If cupids do get to be cheeky to senior angels, it's because they've lots of cheek to go round.

Eventually, in another part of the palace, they came to a door. Before the door was the chamber where the second cupid worked as secretary to the important person they both served. There was a tall stool and, propped up against it, a large diary. The open page of the diary was a mass of entries, every single one of which had been crossed out or ringed with an arrow pointing to the new date on which it was now going to occur. Most had had one or both happen to it several times.

Fug knew that if he had dared to turn the page, the next would have been exactly the same. So would the next, and the next, and the next, with every entry crossed out, postponed, moved or cancelled. Because this was the diary of Love herself. And Love can never keep an appointment.

Fug hovered for a moment before the door of the inner chamber. He was feeling a lot less feisty than he had in the Appeals chamber.

On Earth, there are teachers with really bad tempers. They snap and shout as if the only thing they can do to distract themselves from their inward unhappiness is to make somebody else even more unhappy than they are. They are pretty grim to deal with, but if you get one then at least you know what to expect.

The Angel of Love is not like that.

No, no! The Angel of Love, if she is like a teacher at all, is more the sort who wears sweatbands in class, talks about their divorces and never keeps up with the marking. If you're called up to see the Angel, *anything* could happen, and the smallest 'anything' could turn out to be really big and heavy. And you'll never know if she meant it to be like that or not.

Fug was beginning to sweat. (Being a cupid, he was sweating honey.)

'Good luck,' said the secretary.

Fug swallowed hard and entered the Presence of Love.

Oh, that room! In all the Celestial Palaces there was no other like it. The walls were of Desire, the ceiling was an arch of pure Joy. The drapes were woven of lovers' sighs, the mirrors were Burning Glances, the floor was tiled with Willing Sacrifice. Any mortal who entered would have been overwhelmed at once, melting into notes of music to join the unending harmonies in the air. Even Fug, himself an angel, had to squint a bit in the glory that glowed from the Being within. It was as if he had stepped through the door to find himself within a few feet of the surface of the Sun.

'Hey-y, Fug!' drawled a golden voice. 'Good to *see* you, sweetie – you've been away so long! Have you been neglecting me, you naughty boy?'

'Bin at ther Appeals Board, 'n I?' said Fug,

donning a set of very necessary sunshades. 'They want to see yer 'bout me.'

'Oh dear, really?' said the golden voice. 'What have I done now?'

Fug pulled a face. 'You said to tell 'em, Erry. They din't seem ter like it much.'

'Fug, my darling Fug,' sighed the Voice. 'How many times? We are *Love*. We are patient, we are kind. We are not easily angered. We keep no record of wrongs. Tell me – don't you like the nice job I gave you? Truthfully now?'

Angels are angels, even when they are cupids. They have great respect for the truth. Fug told it.

'Hate the b♥ggers,' he said.

'Then – would you like me to give you another one?' said the angel gently.

'Yeah?' Fug was wary. He would have been very happy to be taken off the Appeals Board. But experience made him cautious. There were some jobs around the Angel of Love he *really* didn't want.

Anything but her secretary, he thought. If it's anything but her secretary, I'll do it. If she wants me to take over as secretary, I defect.

'No need to be shy, Fuggie darling. It's nothing you haven't done before. There's a little job I need done on Earth.' Golden fingers plucked a card from thin air and spun it across the chamber. 'Her.'

The cupid caught it and looked at it coolly, like a pro hit man being handed the details of his next victim.

His coolness warmed up very quickly. 'What's the . . . ? This is a schoolgirl!'

'I believe she is.'

'So what'm I s'posed to do with her?' said Fug sourly. 'Hand her a crush on her Maths teacher?'

Fug was tough and cunning. He had been doing a cupid's work for a long time, down among all those humans with their warm blood and hormones and their great, beating hearts that were about as easy to miss as a barn door. What he liked best were the hard targets – the people who thought they had seen everything, who had little hearts and locked souls and who never believed they could fall in love again. And when he *did* get them, there were consequences that went far beyond the victims themselves. That was what the Department needed him for. In the slang of hit men everywhere, he did the special deliveries.

Early-teen crushes weren't his thing. They were more of a mass-mailing job.

'My dear, sweet Fug,' said The Voice, unrolling the 'r' on 'dear' as if it were a rich carpet. '*Why* do you think I picked you? She's to get "the works", as you like to say. The "full kazooie". Yes?'

That 'Yes' lingered in the air like the dying note of a bell. Fug raised an eyebrow.

'Erry?'

'Don't call me that.'

'Yeah, but what's the deal?'

The Light pulsed slightly, as if to warn the little cupid that he had come very close to using that word 'Why?'

'I have my reasons.'

(OK, thought Fug. So someone had upset the boss. Or done something to get her interested, which came to the same thing only usually a bit worse. Last time he had done a "full kazooie", an empire had fallen and three hundred aunts had been thrown into a snake pit.)

The name on the card said *Sally Jones*.

'I want you to *do* her for me, Fug,' said the angel with a slow, sweet smile. 'Do her properly. Make her an offer she can't refuse.'

5: HARD HAT AREA

In the mind of Sally Jones walked Muddlespot, Messenger of Hell.

He was not a happy little Muddlespot.

He had said he was going to lie down. But he couldn't lie down. He was all jangly. He was depressed.

He knew he should never tire. He should never give up. He should keep coming back, disguised as this, veiled as that, suggesting, whispering, steering, ready for those moments when Sally was weak and using every one.

It was just that she never was.

The pathways of her thoughts spread in all directions. They ran under high, arched ceilings, up flights of broad steps and through many-sided chambers that opened onto more corridors down which the perspectives dwindled towards infinity. The walls were made of crystal that pulsed with gentle colours. Muddlespot could see through them. He could even see through floors, to other chambers and corridors far above his head, or many, many levels below his feet. It was dizzying. Looking down through a hundred and fifty different layers of assorted Facts made his stomach tingle.

There were slogans and mottos and signs up on the walls. Some were about the way Sally wanted things done in her mind. They said things like PLEASE WALK ON THE LEFT or HURRY UP, YOU'RE NEEDED.

Others said things like ASK NOT WHAT MISS SMITH CAN DO FOR YOU BUT WHAT YOU CAN DO FOR MISS SMITH. (Miss Smith was the new Art teacher at Darlington High. Muddlespot had tried telling Sally that she was hopeless. Sally said yes, she knew. That was the point.)

In Sally's mind there were war rooms with charts and maps upon the tables, where steely-eyed, square-shouldered thoughts gathered to take reports, write letters to important people and plan appeals for Operation Save The World. The thoughts wore green uniforms with rank badges in the shape of oak leaves.

They moved purposefully and spoke in short, clipped voices like crack troops who knew that, whatever the odds, they were going to win.

In the corridor below Muddlespot's feet, Sally's French thoughts were knocking off their shift and returning to their rooms. There were smiles among them and a sense of a job well done. They wished each other cheerful goodbyes and disappeared through doors marked Nouns, Subjunctives, Irregular Verbs etc. The German and Spanish thoughts and the Japanese club thoughts lived in other corridors around the mind. They were all kept separate from each other. No mingling was allowed. No way was Sally going to go looking for a word like *saucisson* and find a *Würst* popping up instead. That sort of thing didn't happen to her.

There was a list on the wall. It was headed 'One Thousand Things To Do With My Life.' There were exactly a thousand things on the list. Some of them even had ✓s against them. 'Save the World' didn't have a ✓ yet but the way things were going it might not be much longer.

She had everything sorted out and in its place. She had Dates, Must-do's and Should-do's. She had libraries of Things I Know. She had fountains of

Generosity, gardens of Patience and an entire lighting system of Hope with bulbs that *never* blew. Her mind was built upon space, purpose and clarity. And the greatest of these was clarity.

'Boo,' said Muddlespot sulkily.

He shuffled past another war room. This one was working on Operation End World Poverty. The guys in there looked as though they were winning too. If Muddlespot had had something to kick he would have kicked it.

He skirted the Reading Corridors carefully. The normal rules of Sally's mind (space, purpose etc) did not seem to apply so much to the Reading Corridors, which were dark and narrow and the nearest thing her brain had to a rough end of town. They tended to turn sharp corners so you couldn't see what was waiting round them. Doors and little windows opened on these passages, and from behind them came strange sounds, music maybe, and the noise of hidden feasting, or perhaps screams and cries of battle. Some very queer things lived down there, and sometimes came out. Whenever you found something unexpected in Sally's mind, the chances were that it had wandered out of the Reading Corridors. It was an unsettling place. Muddlespot could never quite escape the feeling that he himself might somehow have come from there, even though he knew with every part of his scientific and rational being that he had been created when someone had hit someone else with a brass hammer in the City of Pandemonium far below, and that he had flown in here on a batskin airplane with squadrons of enraged doves on his tail. Sally had been reading *Paradise Lost* at the time.

He came to the Rules.

They were written into a wall of transparent crystal. When you moved around and looked at them from the other side, you could still read them because the lettering wasn't backwards. And every thought in Sally's mind knew what they said.

The First Rule was this:

Be nise to evryone and they wil be hapy.

It had been written very early in Sally's life when her mind had been quite a different place, much smaller and with bright colours and slides and ball parks and things. The words **and they wil be** had been changed several times over the years, first by adding **usuly** and then by more elaborate forms such as *they will be more likely to be* and *it will help them to be* and *more than they otherwise would be* and so on,

66

in the light of experience. Muddlespot had even tried writing in *it will* NOT *make them any more . . .* But the words **Be nise to evryone . . . hapy** were still there underneath it all, carved deep in a childish hand. They always would be, to the end of Sally's life.

The Second Rule had been written in about Year 4. It read:

Do your best at everything because you can.

There had been no amendments. Experience hadn't even tried to argue with that one.

The Third Rule had been added after a rocky couple of months with relationships in Year Eight. It said:

Keep ruls 1 & 2 but dont rub friends faces in it & dont wory 2 much cos they wil probly b OK with u again soon.

Again there were no amendments. Although a little while afterwards the hand of Experience had added a ☺ and a ✔.

'What,' groaned Muddlespot, 'am I supposed to do with this?'

He had tried and tried. He had spent hours whispering to Sally things like 'Did you see the way she looked at you?' and 'Why are they *excluding* you?' and 'They're *only* being friendly because they want you to help them with their homework' etc. It had made no difference at all. Sally liked and was liked by too many people. If things ever went bad with someone she would go off and be with others for a bit. And (see Rule 1) look for a way to make up. Because everybody did like Sally. Even Muddlespot liked her – a bit. As much as his professional duties allowed.

Which made it all very difficult.

'But I'm here all the same,' he snarled, leering at his reflection in a crystal pillar. 'Me, Muddlespot. *Prince* of Evil!'

His reflection leered back at him. The surface of the column was curved. It exaggerated his waist while doing nothing for his height. As he was basically round anyway the effect was not flattering.

He found a flat bit of wall between two powerful-looking statues. Here he studied his reflection again, frowning fiercely and drawing himself up to his full shape (that of a pear on short stilts). 'I was sent for a purpose,' he intoned. 'Hand-picked.'

The statues looked down upon him. The list from which he had been picked had numbered precisely one. The Authority whose hand had done the picking had gone strangely quiet since the Incident of the Cat, the Muffin and the Wonky Oven. As far as Low Command were concerned, Sally was now in the box marked 'Off

Limits' and Muddlespot in the one marked 'On His Own'.

'I wouldn't be here if she didn't want me!' he cried.

'Want me, want me,' whispered the corridors. *But what does she want me* for? The whispers ran away, fading down the aisles and chambers.

Then, just at the moment when they should have died altogether, there was an echo, or a shuffle of movement, round a corner where he could not see.

'Who's there?' said Muddlespot, wondering if he had really heard it.

Silence.

Frowning, Muddlespot went to investigate.

What he didn't want to find was that Low Command had changed their minds about that 'On His Own' label and had sent someone up to replace him. If so, there was going to have to be a quick bit of murder behind the statues, because he was *not* going back downstairs for a career interview. Career interviews with Low Command tended to be painful and when they were over the only career options left would be as (a) somebody's wall ornament, or (b) their mittens. The sort of people Muddlespot worked for did not like failure.

He tensed. He leaped to the corner of the passage, claws bared. The passage was empty.

'Hello?'

In the darkness at the far end, something scuttled.

Warily Muddlespot stole forward. He entered a small octagonal chamber. The light here was tinted just faintly maroon. The chamber too was empty. He listened. He heard nothing.

Or maybe – maybe – the whisper of bare feet, receding quickly down a distant corridor, and a soft explosion of sound that disappeared with it.

It might have been a snigger.

The air had a huge stillness, as if the whole of Sally's being was holding her breath. (Which it very well might be.)

There *was* something in the room: something small, lying in the middle of the floor like a sweet packet that someone had dropped.

Litter, in the mind of Sally Jones? The rules on litter were *very* strict.

It was a folded bit of card. Muddlespot bent to pick it up.

As he did so, the floor shook.

'It's not FAIR!' Billie screamed.

'Yes it is,' said Sally. They were face to face in the kitchen at home. Sally's feet were planted, her arms were folded. She wasn't backing down. Not even when Billie thrust her face, red as a ripe tomato, within centimetres of Sally's own.

'Sweetheart,' Mum pleaded from the sidelines, 'you don't have to invite anyone you don't want to . . .'

'She already has,' said Sally. 'How's Holly going to feel now if you tell her you don't want her after all?'

'But she makes me *sick*! I just look at her and I feel *sick*! All the time I'm sitting at the table with her in school, I'm trying not to throw up! And I've *got* to have her because *Sally's* invited *Kaz*!'

'Kaz is coming,' said Sally. 'I can't uninvite her.'

'No,' said Mum. 'Of *course* Kathy is coming. Billie – why don't you just *talk* to Holly and clear up whatever the matter is? Last week you were best friends . . .'

'*NO!*' shrilled Billie. 'We weren't *ever*! And the trouble with Holly is HOLLY!'

'Oh,' said Mum.

'All right. Tell Holly you don't want her and invite someone else,' said Sally.

'There *is* no one else!'

'What about Josh? He's nice.'

'NO. *BOYS!*' screamed Billie.

'That does it!' fumed the Inner Sally, who wasn't feeling nearly as calm as the Outer Sally was managing to look. 'I'm going to kill her!'

'No you aren't,' said Windleberry, who was being exactly as calm as the Outer Sally, and even had his arms folded and feet planted in the same way.

'Then I hope she kills herself! Why doesn't she?'

'You don't mean that.'

'Don't I? *We'd* all be happier – and so would she!'

They stood side by side, looking out through the great windows which were the Outer Sally's eyes, and which were largely filled with the sight of Billie's red face.

'You're just so *selfish!*' came Billie's voice from outside. 'Selfish-selfish-*selfish*!'

'*I'm* selfish?' screamed the Inner Sally. 'Looked in a mirror lately, have you?'

'I'm not going to uninvite people I've invited,' said the Outer Sally, without raising her voice. 'If you don't want Holly to come, then invite Lauren or someone like that.'

'Well done,' said Windleberry.

'*When* I need your advice . . .' growled the Inner Sally.

'. . . But Lauren won't come if Freda isn't there!'

'Then invite *both* of them, sweetheart,' said Mum. 'Sally won't mind, will you?'

'Not a bit,' said the Outer Sally.

'Can I say "Well Done" again?' said Windleberry.

'She's got one more than me, now,' said Sally. 'I knew she would.'

'You don't mind about that. You said so yourself.'

'I mind that she's got it by shouting and screaming.'

'Greg's not doing the barbecue, is he?' Billie said dangerously.

'He'd like to,' said Mum.

'Seconds out, round two,' said Sally. 'She'll get at Mum about Greg now. She knows they're going through a bad patch.'

'. . . Well, *I* can't do it, sweetheart! I'm not going to have the time. It'll give him something to do . . .' Mum continued.

'But he's so *embarrassing*! He tries to be *cool*. And his hairy *paunch!*'

'Darling – he'll wear a nice plain T-shirt, I promise . . .'

'He should wear a nice plain sign round his neck that says *I Am Embarrassing*.'

'Actually I agree with her there,' said Sally.

. . . He mustn't talk to anybody. He mustn't even *look* at them . . .'

'He's just trying to be friendly . . .'

'Friendly? He makes me *sick*! I just don't understand why you . . .'

'Time to step in,' said the Inner Sally.

'So,' came her own voice from outside. 'Does this mean you're uninviting Holly and inviting Freda and Lauren instead?'

Through the windows onto the world they saw Billie's face swing round upon them like the gun turret of a tank.

'No,' she said. 'I'm going to invite Cassie and Viola.'

'*What?*' cried the Inner Sally.

And the Outer Sally said, 'You're crazy.'

'I'll invite who *I* want to,' said Billie, reddening again. '*You* have.'

'But Cassie and Viola. Won't. Come.'

'It'll just look like we're trying to get in with their group,' groaned the Inner Sally. 'And that'll never happen, unless we invite the twenty coolest sixth-form boys in the county too. Which would be nice, but they wouldn't come either.'

'*YES THEY WILL!!!!*'

'Social suicide,' said the Outer Sally.

'Sally . . .' said Mum. But it was too late.

'You *always* think I'm wrong! You're *always* being snide and mean! And you're *always* talking me down at school . . .'

74

'Why should I? You do it every time you open your mouth.'

'Sally!' said Mum.

'Sally!' said Windleberry.

'What's going on?' said Muddlespot.

He was peeping round the archway into the chamber where the two of them stood. He had wisely swapped his red pillbox hat for a workman's helmet, in case the roof fell or something came flying in through one of the windows. A mind in the middle of a family row is a hard hat area.

'Just another day in the Jones house,' said the Inner Sally bitterly. 'Where've you been? I've really needed you.'

'No, you really haven't,' said Windleberry.

'Tidying up, I think,' said Muddlespot innocently. 'Did anybody drop this?'

Windleberry looked at it.

It was a small, folded piece of card. Inside the fold, crudely-drawn and coloured, was the shape of a pink heart.

Something inside Windleberry went very quiet and cold.

'That?' he said carefully. 'No, I didn't drop that.'

'What is it, then?'

Angels are not allowed to lie.

'It is a heart, crudely drawn and coloured in pink,' Windleberry said.

The voices of the row outside seemed suddenly far away. The taste of old, bad memories flooded into his mouth. He turned away and drew something from the breast pocket of his dinner jacket.

'... I'm calling Viola now. And after that I'm calling Cassie!'

'Kamikaze,' sighed the Inner Sally.

'And you *can't stop me!*'

'And what's that?' said Muddlespot.

'This? – Oh . . .' said Windleberry, putting it back again. 'Something I happened to have with me. Standard issue.'

It had been a small but powerful hand torch. And for a second, as the twins stood face-to-face in the kitchen, something had flickered in Sally's eye. It had been a signal – for anyone who knew how to read it.

'Really?' said Muddlespot, interested.

'Have you got her number?' said Billie.

Tight-lipped, Sally gave her the number.

'That *looked* like a signal,' said Muddlespot.

'Did it?' said Windleberry. He shut his mouth firmly.

But when he checked his hands, they were shaking.

6: THE PINK HEART

The Jones household at night. The girls are in bed. So is Mum, who has taken herself off early with a headache. The only ones awake are Greg, down in the living room watching the football, and Shades the cat, crouched on the landing and sifting the darkness with his yellow eyes.

The house is a vast, shadowed wilderness, tumbled with belongings. Menace is everywhere. It crouches behind the water glass. It waits beyond the pot of skin cream on the bedside table. It watches from between the sheets of homework, piled untidily beside the door.

On Earth, an angel is an idea. Ideas have to fit inside people's heads. So angels have to be very small, and when they step out of the head that houses them they find the world is very large indeed.

There's no truce out here. Inside the mind there may be rules about what happens when you meet with The Enemy. Outside, there are no limits. Eyes may be gouged, heads split, backs stabbed and tongues torn out by the roots. Out here, you must watch every shadow. And when The Enemy appears, you'd better pray you've got him outnumbered.

On a high, flat hilltop (in fact a pile of books), Windleberry waited. He looked out across the sea of chaos that was Billie's room. Billie did not do tidy. Billie had never done tidy. Parents of career teenagers, who thought that nothing could surprise them any more, peeped in on Billie's room from time to time and were impressed. There were clothes, clothes and more clothes upon the floor (every third item was an odd sock). There were books, papers, sweet wrappers, cassettes, CDs, pencils, pens, sharpeners and – oh, more books, some make-up things that possibly she'd forgotten about and (what was this?) an audiotape, her recorder that she didn't play any more, some pictures that at one time she had been going to put into her album but had in fact been left to crumple under the weight of a pile of shoes that were now too small for her. Every flat surface was crowded, and where things didn't get moved around very often the dust would have come up to Windleberry's knees. The house mites ploughed through it like small komodo dragons.

In the darkness, the shelves and the top of the chest of drawers were mountains crowned with forests. The floor was a mass of waves and shapes and canyons, a volcanic surface where huge lakes of molten lava have flowed and cooled and cracked into piles of tortured rock.

'Guard us,' Windleberry murmured, 'from all perils and dangers of this night . . .'

He turned his head slowly, staring into the darkness. He could see little more than outlines. This was partly because he was wearing sunglasses. But he did not take them off. Angels on Earth never do.

'From all evil and mischief. From the crafts and assaults . . .'

Under her blankets, like a mountainside trembling, Billie shifted and sighed in her sleep.

'From lightning and tempest; from battle and murder . . .'

A shape dropped lightly out of the air and landed on two feet on the far side of the book. It strode towards him, darkness moving in darkness. Windleberry straightened.

'From all sedition . . . ?' he said.

'Aw, heck!' came a voice. 'Who're ya kiddin'? No one does that stuff any more.'

'From all sedition,' said Windleberry more firmly.

'Conspiracy, rebellion, from all false doctrine, heresy and schism, from hardness of heart et cetera. That do?'

'Close enough,' said Windleberry coldly. 'Pass, friend . . .'

'Hey, that's nice of you.'

'. . . Though I think you'll find it's *privy* conspiracy.'

'Privy conspiracy? Is it now? Guess that must be the kinda conspiracy that gets worked up in the johns. How ya doin', Wimple?'

It was an angel. Of a sort. It had the square head, the square shoulders, the dinner jacket, the bow tie and the sunglasses. It had the wings. But it also limped a little as it walked. Its mouth twitched and one hand trembled slightly. Its blank, steady gaze was just a shade less steady than it should have been, as if behind the shelter of its sunglasses its eyes were revolving slowly in opposite directions. As if, sometime in the last half hour or so, it had been picked up by the ankles and used to stun a mammoth.

Ismael was Billie's guardian angel. It was one tough assignment.

'I've had a busy day,' said Windleberry coolly. 'What with that scene Billie threw this evening. I guess you were taking time out?'

Ismael pursed his lips. 'I guess so,' he said. 'After she pushed me through a wall a coupla times, yeah, I think I lay down for a bit. And when she had me in the arm lock – you could say I took time out. I'm kinda attached to my arms. I want to stay that way.'

'Pushed you through a wall?'

'I tell ya, Winkie. What she let out this evening was *nothing*. There was plenty more where that came from. Plenty. She's a good kid. But yeah, she's got issues. Is that why you flashed me the light? You want to tell me to make her better? Easy for you to talk . . .'

'Will she behave at the party?'

'Behave? Depends what you mean. But Billie – she kinda swings. She's had her shout so maybe she'll be sweet for a while. She'll be sweet just because she knows everyone's expecting her to shout again. That's how she is.'

'I see.'

'You think you can do better? Try coming over

sometime. I'll sew up my sides so I don't split 'em watching you.'

'Maybe I will. But that's not why I called you out. It's this.' Windleberry handed him the small, folded piece of card.

Ismael opened it. 'Sheesh!' he said in a low voice.

'Have you had one?'

'Nope,' said Ismael, slowly shaking his head. 'Not that I've seen.'

'Sometimes they hide it. So they can say it's been delivered. But the Guardian doesn't find it. And then the first he knows is . . .'

'Sheesh!'

'I'll put in an objection on Sally's behalf,' said Windleberry. 'Wrong time, exams, commitments and so on. But it'll make no difference.'

'Nope. I guess it won't.'

'Keep your eyes open. They're coming.'

'You're sure?'

'Trust me,' said Windleberry. 'I know them.'

Not far away on the same bedside table, two other figures crouched in a cave. The cave was formed by a money pot, some cardboard packaging from a new school shirt, a broken alarm clock and a roulette set that was missing half its counters and hadn't been played in months. Nevertheless it was a cave. Angels may hang out on high hilltops, but to another sort of person, a cave is a reassuring place. It reminds them of home.

Opposite Muddlespot sat the smallest, shabbiest, evillest-looking creature ever to creep down Darlington Row. His eyes were little horizontal slits, somehow bright and black at the same time. His nose was twice the length of his head, curving and pointed like the beak of a wading bird. He wore a battered broad-brimmed hat the same brown colour as his skin and a shapeless, rumpled coat that covered him from his lips all the way down to his toes. His mouth was tiny and sloped a little to one side. When he spoke all his words seemed to drop out of that downward pointing corner, as if they had trickled down his tongue in blobs of yellow spit and then dribbled out under the force of gravity. He looked like the sort of nightmare that a cockroach might get after pigging on bad cheese.

His name was Scattletail. Like Muddlespot he was an agent from Down Below, from the City of Pandemonium. He was the mouthpiece of Low Command in the mind of Billie Jones.

'What it means, kid,' he said to Muddlespot, 'is he's been tipped the Pink Heart.'

'But what does *that* mean?' asked Muddlespot.

Scattletail spat. 'It means cupids.'

'Uh?'

'Cupids. They're another lot of Fluffies.'

('Fluffies' — angels. As in: 'Death to the Fluffies' and other battle cries of the Low Brigade.)

'. . . What they do is get the humans to fall in love with each other. The pink heart is like their calling card. "We will be working in your neighbourhood" kind of thing. They're s'posed to give the other Fluffies notice that they're coming. Guardians don't like it if their humans go falling in love without warning. They don't like it even when they *do* get warning. It's their job to keep humans on the straight an' narrow. But straight an' narrow don't get much of a look-in when a human falls in love. All sorts of funny things start happening. Black becomes white, right becomes wrong. An' they start singing.' He shuddered. 'That's usually the worst part.'

'So this is just between the Fluffies? Nothing to do with us?'

'Ye-es. An' no. It depends. Me 'n Ismael – we have this deal. 'Stead of fighting or arguing, we play at cards.

He wins, he gets to say something to Billie. I win, I do. Keeps it civil. We know where we are. 'S far as either of us know where we are with Billie. But,' – he spat again. Out in the darkness, something sizzled – 'I reckon neither of us'd take it kindly if the cards started flying around or the table started walking or the chairs started chucking themselves. That's what it's like when you get hit. Nothing's where you think it is any more.'

'Hit? Like with a hammer?'

'I've known it. Cupids – they use arrows mostly. But hammers – yep, I've known it. Also harpoons. Knew someone who got done with a wrecking ball once. Anything'll work, as long as it's gold.'

'So – what should I do?'

'Depends. You winning in there?'

Scattletail was a sideways kind of person. He looked sideways, spoke sideways, walked sideways, and he could spit to any angle from about 45° to 120°. He was looking sideways now, with his great nose curving off into the night like a toucan's bill. And his dark little eyes were very, very direct.

Muddlespot shifted a little. 'Of course,' he said.

'Hm?'

'Underneath it all,' Muddlespot insisted. 'In a subtle way.'

'Hm.'

'Oh, I know how it *looks*,' said Muddlespot. 'But that's all part of my plan.'

Muddlespot knew he couldn't keep the true state of affairs quiet for ever. Sooner or later Low Command was going to have to notice what was going on with Sally, and then he'd be replaced and hauled off for that career interview and everything that came with it. His best chance of survival was to get himself transferred to another human first. The recognized way of achieving this was to sneak up on a colleague, disembowel and dismember him in a suitably collegiate fashion and then to take his place. Low Command didn't usually mind if you did that. Most of them had done it themselves at some time or other.

He had already eyed Scattletail's neck and wondered about his chances of getting his talons around it. But Scattletail wasn't just a colleague. He was . . .

. . . Well, not a *friend*, because the sort of people Muddlespot and Scattletail were did not make friends, and anyone trying to make friends with them would be being *most* unwise . . .

But it was reassuring, sometimes, to see him, and to compare notes on cards with pink hearts on them and other things like that. Scattletail had been playing this game for a long time.

Which was probably why he hadn't once turned his back on Muddlespot. Nor had he taken his hands out of his pockets. Scattletail's coat looked as if it had really quite deep pockets. There could be a lot of nasty things down there. Muddlespot wondered what they were.

On the whole, he thought, he'd rather not find out.

'See,' said Scattletail. 'If you're winning, you probably don't want 'em. They just make it more difficult. But if things are running against you some-how, and you need that break, then maybe a quick hit with a golden arrow might do it for you. 'Mazing what can follow from one of those. Lies, tears, battle and murder – you can get the lot.'

'But . . .' said Muddlespot.

'But?'

Muddlespot wriggled a little. 'I've, er, also got a deal, you see. With my opposite number. We keep it local. Just him and me. No interference from outside. We don't let anyone in from Down Below. Not after the, er, Muffin Incident, you remember?'

Scattletail nodded slowly. He remembered all right.

'. . . So, er, *if* he thinks he's winning, and he doesn't want the lies and tears and battle and murder, then he'll say the same applies to people from Above. We shouldn't be letting them in. And he'll expect me to back him up on that.'

'So?'

'So . . .' Muddlespot shrugged helplessly. 'Well, a deal's a deal.'

Scattletail's eyes were on him. They were black and bright and cold. And very, very deep.

'Sure,' he said. And added slowly, 'But a devil's a devil, isn't he?'

'I guess you're right.' Muddlespot sighed. 'I never get used to that bit.'

He looked at his toes. He was more nervous than he dared to admit. Windleberry was strong. During the 'Muffin Incident' he had gone thirteen rounds with Muddlespot's boss – a *very* formidable person – and had come out on top. It was definitely in Muddlespot's interest that there should be a few rules about how things were done inside Sally's head. He would have felt a lot happier about binning the 'Keep It Local' rule if he could have known which other rules were going to get binned with it. He particularly wanted to keep the one about 'No Smiting'. The 'No Eye-Gouging',

'No Knee-capping' and 'No Wedgies' rules were also important, he thought.

And yet – it all started from Sally. In a way, Windleberry was strong because Sally *wanted* him to be strong. And for some reason Muddlespot could not fathom, Sally also wanted Muddlespot to be Muddlespot. There was a place for him in her mind. It just wasn't a very big one. At the moment.

But if things were to change . . .

Into his mind stole the idea of Sally – the maddeningly perfect Sally – caught in the grip of emotions that she could neither control nor understand. And then – the sly word here, the quick trip there . . . His power growing. His enemy floundering, overwhelmed . . .

Without being aware of it, he had begun to rub his hands.

'Battle and murder, you say?'

'Trust me. An' that's not the worst of it.'

'No?'

'You get some dam' repetitive singing as well.'

7: THE HIT

They did the party in the rec, which was a sloping patch of threadbare grass surrounded by bushes on the edge of the Bullwater Housing Estate. It boasted some swings, some kids' climbing frames and the world's shortest football pitch, but it also had a couple of barbecues that you could book and some tables where you could eat your picnic. Greg brought the meats up in a cool-basket and started to make smoke. Mum must have had a word with him, because although it was sunny and hot he was wearing a shirt and did not try to talk to anybody. He did not have a sign hung around his neck saying 'I am Embarrassing' but he looked as though there might have been one there invisibly.

The friends came. Cassie and Viola didn't come,

because of course they were never going to, and Freda and Lauren, who probably would have done, happened to be going to the beach with Freda's family that day. So Billie had invited Holly after all and everybody else in the house had carefully Not Said Anything.

So who was there, wearing what, and what did they bring?

Kaz came wearing a T-shirt and shorts, and she brought Billie a water pistol and Sally a book.

Annie came wearing a party dress and a sparkly feather boa, and she brought both twins pink spangly birthday cards with gift vouchers inside them.

Eva came in jeans and a plain white top, and she brought Billie a pendant with a pale blue plastic stone in it and Sally a book.

Ellen also came in jeans and a plain white top, and since her hair was dark and short like Eva's poor Greg got them mixed up and everybody yelled at him. Ellen brought both girls chocolates, which just HAD to be eaten there and then because they were melting in the sun.

Lolo had come straight from her riding lesson, and she was wearing a striped T-shirt and jodhpurs. She brought Billie a framed picture (of a horse) and Sally a book (about horses).

Imogen came in skin-tight jeans and a blouse knotted at the waist. She gave Billie some quality paint-brushes and Sally a copy of *Madame Bovary* by the French writer Flaubert, which was a good try even though Sally had in fact already read it. Imogen wasn't really a friend of either twin. She was good at music with super-pushy musical parents, but apart from that the one thing she wanted in all the world was to be in with Cassie and Viola. This was a tough one because she had frizzy hair and slightly pop eyes and the first thing you had to do if you wanted to be one of Cassie's set was to look perfect in every way. But Imogen's uncle had an Aston Martin and was happy to give rides, so they sort of allowed her as a hanger-on.

Of course, by the time Billie had asked her, it had already been clear that Cassie and Viola would not be coming. But Billie had wanted the one-person-extra that she had won in the argument so she had said 'and I've asked Cassie and Viola' in a way that made it sound as though they definitely were. Now Imogen had got to the rec bearing presents and found they weren't. This made everyone feel awkward from the start (except Billie).

Holly came in a dark blue top with white jeans and

she bought the best presents of all, i.e. two ten-pound notes.

Out in the street by the gate Charlie B and Rich and David were doing wheelies on their bicycles. Charlie was round in face and body. Rich and David were lean and dark and shaggy. They were all in Sally's and Billie's class, and they hooted and rang their bells at the girls as they came bowling over the speed bumps, but they didn't ask why they hadn't been invited. It never occurred to them that they might have been.

'Cover your arc,' said Windleberry tersely. 'Left eye, left ear. I'll take the right. Got that?'

'Sure,' said Muddlespot. He said it with a grunt because he thought it made him sound tough.

(Windleberry had caught him in one of the corridors of Sally's mind and – with a friendly grip on his elbow – had told him that there might be some callers from another part of Heaven. Muddlespot had said, 'Oh.'

Windleberry had said that there had been a serious mistake and that these callers had not been authorized and that their presence in Sally's mind or anywhere near Sally's vicinity would be a very bad thing. Muddlespot had said, 'I see.'

Windleberry had asked whether Muddlespot

remembered their agreement about no interference from outside. Muddlespot had said, 'I do.'

Windleberry had then said it might be necessary to discourage the presence of these callers in very strong terms and asked if, bearing in mind their agreement, Muddlespot was willing to help do some discouraging. Muddlespot had said 'I am,' and had added a specially innocent smile which he had been practising ever since his talk with Scattletail.

Windleberry had looked at him very hard. But he could not decide whether Muddlespot was actually lying, or whether his misgivings were simply because Muddlespot was a devil and therefore not to be trusted about 99% of the time whatever. In the end he had decided that for Sally to get hit by the cupids was no more in Muddlespot's interest than it was in his, and therefore this might really be the 1% of the time when Muddlespot could be expected to help.

Bad bet.)

Muddlespot fully intended to *look* as though he was helping. To prove his good intentions he had dressed himself like a bouncer. He had put on a black dinner jacket, black tie and dark sunglasses. He had also added several rolls of cloth under his dinner jacket to make his shoulders look big. There would be no unwanted gate-crashers here, thank you, his pose said. No cupids. Certainly not without wearing a tie.

Then he looked at what Windleberry was wearing. And he wondered if maybe he had not got the full picture of what these cupids were about.

Windleberry was in full military combat dress and webbing. His cheeks were daubed with fierce camouflage stripes. His battle helmet was covered with netting, which was was stuffed with sticks and straw. He clanked with knuckle-dusters and tripwires and ninja darts and handcuffs and stun-guns and blowpipes and man-traps and radio beacons and night scopes and arrest warrants and electronic tags. He'd wanted to arm himself with a fiery sword, a lance of lightning and a Mark III Holy Rocket-Propelled Grenade Launcher, but Sally didn't like loud noises and wouldn't allow anything that might make one. If it came to close quarters he was trusting in his lead-lined baseball bat.

He also had a whole bundle of forms already filled out so that he could report instantly and in triplicate all the things that he reckoned he was going to have to do here. Whatever happened next, there would be a row about it in Heaven. There might well be a visit from the Celestial Inspection Angels (CIA) to whom all parties would have to explain themselves. Windleberry knew about Celestial Inspections. They were conducted on the basis that everybody was an angel and angels must at all times tell the Truth, the Whole Truth and Nothing But The Truth. Therefore if, as an angel, you find yourself being inspected, the one thing you've got to do is to get your Truth in First.

'Remember,' hissed Windleberry to Muddlespot. 'We work together, got that?'

'Right,' said Muddlespot, and grunted.

'I'm counting on you,' said Windleberry.

'Right,' said Muddlespot, and grunted again.

'You seem a bit tense, you guys,' said the Inner Sally. 'What's up?'

Windleberry could not lie, so he said nothing.

'Oh, nothing,' said Muddlespot, who could.

'This lot will keep me going for a bit,' said Sally, looking quickly through the pile of books that her guests had given her.

'And look out for the nose,' whispered Windleberry.

'The nose?' said Muddlespot.

'It can start with a scent,' said Windleberry darkly. 'Rose petals, usually.'

'I think I'm going to learn a few things I didn't know about horses,' said Sally.

Smoke drifted across the rec, bearing with it mouth-watering smells. The girls were all sitting on the grass in the sun, listening to music playing on some speakers someone had brought along.

'I can't believe he got us mixed up,' said Eva to Ellen. 'We don't even *look* the same!'

'He's so embarrassing,' grumbled Billie.

'He's cooking for me,' said Ellen happily. 'I can live with it.'

'I think Mum's going to ditch him soon,' said Billie.

Imogen was sitting a little to one side, sulking because Cassie and Viola were not going to appear. Down in the road the riders whooped as they rode full tilt over the speed bumps. There were more of them now.

'Boys at eleven o'clock,' said Windleberry. 'Coming in for another pass.'

'She shouldn't have said that,' said Sally.

'Roger out,' said Muddlespot, because it seemed to be the right sort of thing to say.

'Anything your side?'

'Er – a rose bush?'

'Keep your eye on it.'

'I am.'

It was about three metres away, a mix of yellow and orange and peach-coloured heads, nodding easily in the sun. Muddlespot *thought* he had seen a movement there – a suspicious twitch of a petal that surely should not have twitched. He watched it very closely in case it twitched again. His skin prickled. If it was what he thought it was, then he was going to look very carefully somewhere else. But first he wanted to know if this was the right place not to look.

'It's not like it's any of *their* business,' said Sally. 'Poor Greg.'

Billie was in a good mood. Ismael knew that because his cards were strong. There were aces when he needed them, nines when he needed them, and when he went for the five-card hand he got the obliging fours and threes.

Even so, he did not drop his guard. Billie could change like the weather in April – all sunny one minute and storms the next. She was drifting around the central chamber of her mind, humming the music and laughing from time to time. But she was also restless. She couldn't keep still. He would look up at her and find that she mentally changed the colour of her party dress, or was wearing a different scrunchy in her hair. Big spangly bracelets appeared on her arms. The next minute they were gone.

Opposite him sat Scattletail, hunkered over his cards. He was betting small – bidding for a yawn or a snarky comment but nothing more than that. He was waiting for his luck to turn. His eyes never changed, whatever the run of play.

'Do you think this party needs livening up?' said the Inner Billie wistfully.

'Hey, honey – take a hand if you're bored.'

Ismael had to say that, though he knew it was a risk. It was how things worked in Billie's mind. Billie made a show of thinking about it. Then she said, 'OK – deal me in.'

'Blackjack?' Ismael wanted to keep the game as it was. The less change now, the better.

'Texas Holdem,' said Billie firmly, sitting down and putting on a cowboy hat. 'Deal me in, pardner.'

Flick, flick, flick went the cards. Scattletail sat up. He drew his seat closer to the table.

*

'Immy, are you OK?' asked Annie.

'I'm fine,' said Imogen. Her voice was muffled because she was lying with her head pillowed on her arms. But her tone made it absolutely clear that she wasn't. It had been dumb to invite her, and dumber still to have tried to invite Cassie and Viola. Everyone knew that. Except Billie.

'Let her be,' whispered Holly.

The best hope for Imogen, Sally decided, was that she should get a boyfriend. That would cure her of wanting to be with Cassie and Viola. But – see (a) frizzy hair et ceteror and (b) the generally low standard of available boys – it might take some doing. Someone might have to play cupid.

I love you love you love you love you sang the speakers. The warm air stirred the leaves in the bushes and set the rose heads nodding.

Right in Muddlespot's line of vision, something moved.

It looked like a head, peeping cautiously out of a crown of rose petals. It was round and seemed to be attached to a pair of shoulders. But it was black and blind and . . .

No, it *was* a head. It was a head wearing a balaclava.

The rest of the body – as far as Muddlespot could see – wasn't wearing anything. There was a shoulder, a gleam of a fat little chest and a pudgy forearm. The hand of the arm held a bow.

'Anything your side?' said Windleberry.

Muddlespot licked his lips. Then, very determinedly, he looked away from the rose. He fastened his eyes on the plant beside it. It was a gladiolus, with straight green leaves and dark red flowers.

'No,' he said. 'Nothing at—'

There was one in the gladiolus too. This one also had a bow. And a balaclava.

There were *three* in the cypress beyond.

Muddlespot backed a bit. He couldn't help it. The sight of them unnerved him. The way they moved – quickly, ruthlessly, flitting from one patch of cover to the next, so fast that by the time his head turned to follow the movement they were in cover again, and while he was still trying to pick them out another had moved – and each time nearer to him.

He knew it wasn't him they were after. But even so, he backed again. He badly wanted something to hide behind.

'Though it's a while since I, er, since I had my eyes tested . . .'

'What . . . ?' said Windleberry.

'*Go, Go, Go!*' cried a voice, deep as a bullfrog spitting pebbles. And they were everywhere – pouring in through the windows in a wave of chubby bodies wearing nothing but balaclavas. Arms lifted. Bows bent.

'Hey . . .' said the Inner Sally.

'HAI!' roared Windleberry, leaping forward in a karate pose.

'. . . Don't point those things at me!' said Sally.

Twang, twang, twangatwangatwang! went the bows. Windleberry's arms moved in a blur, chopping left and right. Golden arrows tumbled from the air.

'Muddlespot!' cried Windleberry. 'Attack!' He dived forwards.

'Oh – er – yes!' said Muddlespot. He lifted his fists and faced the one corner of the room where there didn't happen to be any cupids. 'Come on, you!' he shouted aggressively. 'You want some? You want some?'

'*Reload!*' yelled the lead cupid. '*Spread out!*'

Punt! went Windleberry's toe.

'*Weeeeeeeeeeeeeeeeeeeeeeeeeeeeeeh!!!*' went a cupid, disappearing out through the window at about twice the speed it had come in.

'Muddlespot!' cried Windleberry desperately. 'Take the two on the left!'

'The left,' repeated Muddlespot. 'Right.' He faced *right* and found himself nose to nose with a rather surprised cupid who had been expecting him to go the other way.

'B▼gger ▼!!!' said the cupid.

'Oh, sorry,' said Muddlespot. 'My mistake.'

'*Hai, Hai!*' cried Windleberry, fighting the Good Fight as only he could. Cupids were flying in all directions – mostly without wanting to. He had one by the ankles and was using it as a club. It was swearing horribly.

'Everything – you say,' gasped Windleberry, 'will be – taken down and used in evidence . . . Sally – *duck!*'

'Quack,' said Sally, and dropped to the floor. Windleberry hurled the cupid through the air. It caught the two remaining cupids and knocked them off their feet just as they loosed their shots. One arrow went high into the air, whistling up out of the great window and into the wide world. The other hissed over Windleberry's shoulder and—

'OW!' cried Muddlespot.

'I'll have that,' said Windleberry, disarming the stunned cupids. 'And those. Now be *off* with you.'

He tossed them one after another out of the window.

'What did they want?' said the Inner Sally.

'To change your life,' said Windleberry. He took a cupid bow, tested it, and made to break it over his knee. Then he stopped himself and put it down thoughtfully.

'I could have handled them,' said Sally.

'So many people think that.'

'What's the matter with him?'

In the far corner of the chamber lay Muddlespot, flat on his back with his arms wide. He was not moving.

'There were a lot of arrows flying about,' said Sally doubtfully. 'Do you think he stopped one?'

They bent over the recumbent form.

Feeling just a little self-conscious, Windleberry patted his foe gently on the cheek. 'Are you all right?'

Muddlespot opened his eyes.

'My win,' said Ismael, relieved. 'Everybody take a look round and see what a fine day it is. Be thankful for it.'

'Sure,' said Scattletail sourly. 'Done that. Now deal again.'

Flick, flick, flick went the cards.

WheeeeeeeeeeeeeeeeTHUMP! went something else.

'Erk!' went Billie.

She stiffened. Slowly she slumped forward onto the table. Ismael stared at her. There was something, he saw, sticking out of her back. He blinked at it once, twice, before the things his eyes were seeing made sense in his shocked brain. With a horrible, cold, crawling feeling he recognized it for what it was – the butt of a golden arrow, protruding from between her shoulder blades.

There was even a calling card attached to it. With a pink heart.

'Holy cow!' he gasped.

Scattletail was also staring at it, mouth gaping. 'Where did *that* come from?'

'Billie? Speak to us, Billie – are you OK?'

Slowly Billie lifted her head. Her eyes were wide. They were shining. Her lips broke slowly into the most glorious smile. One look at her was enough to tell Ismael that it was far, far too late to do anything.

'It's him,' she whispered. 'It's him!'

She ran to the great windows like the Lady of Shalott running to see Sir Lancelot ride between the barley-sheaves.

'Er – who exactly . . . ?' Scattletail sounded nervous.

'*Him!*'

*

A yell rang out across the rec. The girls looked up, startled. None of them had noticed that Billie had wandered a little way from the group.

'Hey,' she called, down to the street where the boys were wheeling to and fro. 'Hey, *Tony!*'

The boys were looking up at her. Everyone was looking at her. She scampered down the field to the fence. Out in the road Tony Hicks, demigod of Year Twelve, skidded to a halt.

'Hey, Tony!' said Billie, holding the railings and bouncing up and down. 'You want to come in? Come in and have something to eat!'

Tony had joined the Year Nine boys riding up and down the road because he had nothing else to do (except homework, which could wait!). He had jumped the bumps a few times and found it was harder than he had hoped to get both wheels off the ground. Plus, it was like getting kicked in the butt every time his rear wheel hit. Jeez! The Year Nine boys seemed to like it. They pedalled themselves towards the bumps harder and harder and howled with glee as their bikes bounced them into the air. They looked as if they could go on doing it for ever.

Here, on the other hand, was Billie. He didn't

know her too well but she seemed to be a nice kid and obviously pleased to see him. That was cool. Lots of girls of all ages at Darlington High were keen on him. He was dimly aware that certain people felt they had rights over him, and that others would interfere with him at their peril. But he owed no one any loyalty. Like a benign spirit, he was at peace with all forms of lower life and bestowed himself wherever he pleased. Besides, there seemed to be sausages on offer.

'Sure,' he said, and leaned his bike up against the railings. He let himself in through the gate.

He even let Billie take his hand. He saw no harm in it.

'Oh,' said Ellen under her breath. 'Em. Gee.'

'*I* thought he was with Viola,' said Annie.

'Trouble,' said Eva.

'*I* thought,' whispered Sally, 'she said no boys.'

They watched the couple walking up to the barbecue, arm in arm. Beside them Imogen sat up. Her frizzy hair was untidy. Her face was blotched from resting on her arms. She stared blearily at the scene below her. 'What's she doing?' she asked.

'Viola's going to go ballistic,' whispered Lolo.

There was a short silence.

Viola wasn't really older than anyone else in the class. She just acted that way. So did Cassie. So did all that group – Millie, Tara . . .

And there was no way Imogen wasn't going to tell them.

'I think I'm going to have flu on Monday,' said Annie in a small voice. 'Good luck, the rest of you.'

'I,' said Holly, 'am leaving for Mongolia'.

Something had hit Muddlespot in the chest, so hard that it had hurt. He remembered that clearly. He was surprised to find that it had stopped hurting almost at once.

He could still feel it, though. He could feel something – different. It was as if all the scenery had just waited for that instant in which his eyes were closed, and had swapped itself around subtly so that he could not quite see what had happened or how. Everything seemed to be brighter. Snatches of pale gold mist hung in the corners of his sight. He was lying on his back, looking up into the face of . . .

Windleberry.

And suddenly everything was clear.

His fear had gone. His hate . . . Hate? Could he possibly have been *hating* Windleberry? No! He had been hating himself. He could see that now. He had been confused. He had blinded himself to what was real. But now he could see. He knew the truth at last.

'Windleberry,' he breathed.

The sound of the angel's name from his own lips stirred his heart. Something inside his chest opened, slowly, gloriously, like a flower. The air was full of music. There was a spring in his muscles, a lightness. In that instant he could have leaped buildings or flown to mountain tops. There was newness and hope. There was a reason for everything, and it was before his very eyes.

'Windleberry,' he repeated. He smiled a huge smile. 'My *hero*.'

'What?' said Windleberry.

'Windleberry – I've always admired you! Even as I've been your enemy. I want you to know this. There's been this feeling for you inside me . . .'

'Oh no . . .' said Windleberry. He tried to step back, but Muddlespot rolled and caught him by the ankle, hugging his foot to his cheek.

'Be mine!' he cried. 'I cannot live without you!'

'Let go!' said Windleberry desperately. 'This is . . . we could both be summoned for this!'

'Why should we care?' moaned Muddlespot, who was clinging to Windleberry's ankle. 'As long as we have each other? Oh Windleberry – let's run away together!'

'We're in trouble, guys,' said Sally, who wasn't looking at them.

'Trouble!' exclaimed Windleberry. 'Do you have any idea how *embarrassing* this is?' He tried to free himself, but all he succeeded in doing was dragging Muddlespot bodily across the floor. 'Let me go!' he cried. 'Unhand me, fiend! Or I shall Smite Thee, yay verily!'

'I'm already smitten, thank you,' said Muddlespot, kissing Windleberry's toe.

Sally was watching the sunlit world outside, where Billie had coaxed Tony into lying on the grass and letting her feed him a sausage.

'This,' she murmured, 'means war.'

Windleberry glanced sourly down at his ankle. 'You think you've got problems?' he said.

8: WAR!

Viola got the call from Imogen. She listened. She rang off. Pale and hard-eyed, she stared into the mirror for a long thirty seconds. Then she rang Tony's mobile.

'...YOU'RE DUMPED!'

'Huh?' said Tony.

The next thing was that everyone had to go to school on Monday morning. Except for Annie, who somehow managed to persuade her parents that she really did have flu.

As luck would have it, Sally and Billie passed Viola and Cassie and Tara at the school gates. The three stopped talking as they approached. Their eyes followed Billie. Billie walked past with her nose in the air.

'Hi,' said Sally, as cheerfully as she could.

None of them answered.

There was an envelope stuck with Blu-Tack to the door of Billie's locker.

'Don't open that,' said Sally.

Billie scowled. She opened it. She read it. She went pink.

'Who's it from?' asked Annie, looking over her shoulder.

'Typed,' hissed Billie. 'And unsigned.'

Holly read some of it. 'Ouch,' she said. 'You should show that to Mr Singh.'

'They'll expect that,' said Billie. Deliberately she tore the letter to small shreds. 'Right. If that's the way they want it . . .'

'Stay out of trouble,' said Sally.

'I don't care about trouble,' said Billie.

'No,' said Sally. 'You don't, do you?'

In English Sally shared a table with Rich and Charlie B. She had been put with them at the start of the spring term to reduce the number of riots in that corner of the room. Of course, anyone sitting anywhere close to Rich was likely to get caught in the unending crossfire of flying Blu-Tack, pencil sharpeners, erasers, gumballs and rolled-up paper pellets that he inhabited as a fish inhabits water. Also, somebody had once left a drawing pin on her chair rather than his by mistake. This was the sort of thing that happened to Sally.

Just for today, however, being with the boys did mean that she was safe from some other things. It was as if the UN had flown in a separation force of foreign peacekeepers just for her. They were chaotic and unruly but mostly well-meaning. And they kept the war at a distance.

Others weren't so lucky. Holly was sharing a table with Imogen. Holly had always been Billie's staunchest supporter. No matter what Billie did or said, Holly would find a word to say in her favour. Life, she said, was never dull when Billie was around. (Which was what had made it so awkward when Billie hadn't wanted to invite her to the rec.)

There was no question where Imogen's loyalties were going to lie.

So here were two ordinary and perfectly likeable girls having trouble breathing the same air. Neither spoke to the other. They worked head-down in white, tight-lipped silence. The temperature on that table must have been a good ten degrees lower than the rest of the room. And sitting between them was little Minnie Stubbs. She looked from one to the other with a face that said *What's got into you?*

Stay out of it, Minnie, thought Sally. For your own sake.

Then it got worse. Mr Kingsley handed out copies of a poem called *The Hound of Heaven* and asked them to read it through.

> I fled Him down the nights and down the days;
> I fled Him down the arches of the years;
> I fled Him down the labyrinthine ways
> Of my own mind . . .

Sally scanned to the bottom of the first page. She turned over. Her hand went up. So did half a dozen others. Eventually Mr Kingsley noticed.

'What *is* it?' he said (in the voice of a querulous parrot).

'The second page is blank.'

'Oh!' said Mr Kingsley, as if this were the class's fault. He checked Eva's paper, and then Lolo's. Then he had to admit defeat. 'It must be the photocopier,' he said. 'It's done them one-sided.'

Everyone looked at him.

'I'll have to copy them again. Just read the first page over and think about what it means. I won't be a moment.'

. . . **All things betray thee**, said the poem, **who betrayest Me.**

He wouldn't be a moment.

He said.

There were several photocopiers in the school. They had been bought at different times and sat in different places, but they had three things in common:

   a. They were all old.
   b. They always had at least one person ahead of you when you arrived with your photocopying.
   c. They always knew when you were in a hurry.

They liked people who were in a hurry. They saved their worst faults and paper jams just for the poor woman who had to get her copying done *now*, so they could bask in the flow of abuse and cries of pain that followed. It did something for them. Heaven knew what. Maybe they were secretly hoping that whoever it was would turn into a crazed axe-murderer and would end their miserable existences with a few deranged chops. Maybe the whole thing was an elaborate suicide pact among photocopiers. Whatever the reason, they certainly worked at it.

Maybe they knew there was a war on in 9c.

Mr Kingsley didn't.

The minutes ticked past. The buzz of an unsupervised class rose. The boys started taking pot shots at each other. A rubber band flew past Sally's ear.

'What a lovely day it is,' said Minnie brightly. 'Smile, everybody . . .'

Minnie! thought Sally desperately. Just stay *out*!

'I'm building a wall,' chirrupped Minnie. She began to make bricklaying motions in the air between Holly and Imogen. 'I'm Build-ing a Wa-all . . .'

Whatever Imogen said to Minnie it was short with about three 'S's in it. Sally heard them hiss across the room. She saw Minnie go still for a moment. Her shoulders seemed to shrink. She looked down.

Holly said something to Imogen across her. Imogen ignored it.

All three of them were quiet for the rest of the lesson.

When it ended (about six minutes after Mr Kingsley

finally returned with the photocopying) and everyone rose to go, Sally saw that Minnie was crying.

At break Holly met them in the corridor. 'Have you checked your games bag?' she asked.

'No, why?'

'Someone's taken my shin pads.'

'Mine too,' said Eva.

Sally and Lolo checked their bags. Their shin pads were also missing.

'It's hockey this afternoon. With Miss Tackle.'

Sally thought about it. Just standing there, it felt as if her shins were already beginning to throb. 'Ow,' she said.

'It's mean!' Holly was almost spitting. 'It's so . . . *bitchy!*'

'Why us?' wailed Eva. 'We didn't invite him.'

'Guilt by association,' said Sally.

'What does that mean?'

'It means that Viola wants as many victims as she can get.'

'But it's not as if we've done anything to *her* . . .'

Viola screamed.

She was about ten metres away down the corridor, standing at her locker with Imogen and Cassie. All three of them jumped back shrieking. Viola's bag tumbled to the floor, spilling books, water bottles, deodorants, comb, make-up, calculators and pins across the linoleum. Viola's face was green.

Just at that moment Billie walked by. Viola turned on her.

'A mouse!' she hissed. 'A mouse!'

'They get everywhere, don't they?' said Billie innocently. She kept walking. As she passed Sally and the others she clenched her fists and whispered a fierce, 'Yes!'

'You idiot,' Sally said. Billie ignored her.

A small crowd had gathered around the fallen bag. Viola was trembling. Cassie and Imogen had their arms around her. Sally swallowed hard and went over.

There it was, lying in the middle of the things that Viola had spilled on the floor: a poor brown fleck of fluff with a pale belly, a tail, claws and little yellow teeth. It was quite dead. Viola must have been looking for something in her bag (which was like a smart leather handbag, only sized up so that it was big enough to carry books and stuff) and her fingers would have closed on it, and she would have pulled it out to see what it was. Ouch.

'I'll deal with it,' sighed Sally. She took a tissue

from her pocket, dropped it over the dead thing and picked it up. Cassie and Imogen just glared at her. She felt their eyes on her back as she carried it away.

'What's the matter?' said Mr Singh, emerging from his office.

'A dead mouse,' said Sally.

Mr Singh, who was Head of Year, frowned. He had a turban, a big black beard and big bushy eyebrows. If frowning had been a sport he could have competed at national level.

'Where did you find it?'

Sally knew a moment of inner struggle. It went like this.

WINDLEBERRY: You must tell the truth.

SALLY: I can't dump on Billie.

WINDLEBERRY: The sooner the teachers know, the sooner they'll put a stop to it.

SALLY: I can't dump on Billie.

MUDDLESPOT: I'm sure we should listen to Windleberry, Sally: He's right. And he's wise and clever and handsome and gracious and—

WINDLEBERRY: Shut UP!

MUDDLESPOT: Say you love me.

WINDLEBERRY: No! Just keep watching for cupids!'

'Lying on the floor in the corridor,' said Sally.

SALLY: Don't look at me like that! He asked me where I
              found it!
WINDLEBERRY: I'm disappointed, Sally.

'We shouldn't have those in the building,' said Mr
Singh. 'Take it to the janitors and tell them where it
was. They'll know what to do.'

He was right, Sally thought. There shouldn't be
any mice in the school. There *weren't* any mice in
the school. Janitors and cooks and cleaning staff and
whole legions of exterminators leaped into action at
the first sign of a whisker. The Food Tech Block was
regularly closed for checks. The fastest way to make a
deputy head faint was to utter the word 'infestation'.
The PTA was said to be funding ultrasonic vermin
repellents at strategic points around the building.

So how had Billie got hold of one?

Fug was lurking in the cover of a loo-roll tube. 'Boss?'
he said. 'Hello, boss?'

'Hey, Fu-u-ug!' drawled the honey-thick voice from
on high, via the golden trumpet that sat on top of Fug's
communication kit. 'How a-a-are you, my lovely?'

120

Fug winced. It sounded like the boss was having one of her moods again.

'Mission accomplished. Results Positive. Awaiting Recall.'

'You made the hit?'

'Sure we did. The Jones Kid is down.'

There was a short pause at the far end, during which Fug scowled warningly at his troops. *I said 'The Jones Kid', his eyebrows semaphored. I didn't say which Jones Kid. And if any of you want to go back and have Mr Windleberry reshape your faces with his fists, all you have to do is speak up now.*

None of the cupids spoke.

The Angel of Love let out her breath. '*That's go-o-o-od,*' she said. '*You're such a sweetie, Fug. You did everything I meant for her?*'

'The full kazooie, like you said.'

'*Any effects yet?*'

'Boss — it's war down here, I tell you.'

'*Good job!*' said the angel, suddenly brisk. '*OK, Fug, no hanging around now. There's work to do. Kick arse and get your boys back up here right away.*'

'Will do, boss.'

'*War — I like it! You're a darling, Fug. You're a sugar-pie.*'

The connection cut. Gingerly, Fug stood up.

He rubbed his buttocks, one of which, courtesy of Windleberry's toe, was mostly black and the other mostly blue. Both were about half again the size they should be.

Kick arse?

Been enough of that already, he thought.

Sally spent the second half of lunch break in the library. She made sure she sat in the direct line of sight of Mrs Collins, so no one could interfere with her. The library was quiet, except for the gentle ticking of the clock on the wall as it counted the seconds until break ended and the hockey-pitch massacre could begin. She needed something to distract her, so she was working on her extra essay for Mr Kingsley. For that she had to be able to write about another Shakespeare. The one she had chosen was called *Troilus and Cressida*.

It was, as Mr Kingsley himself had said, a difficult and nasty story, set thousands of years ago when the Greeks were Ancient Greeks and pretty well nobody else was around. The sixth-formers had done it as their school play last year, and they had recruited Sally to be assistant props manager, because when it came to keeping lots of different items in order and making sure the right person had them at the right time she was a lot more reliable than most sixth-formers (who all wanted to be onstage, anyway). So Sally sort of knew what it was about, without having to read it. Plus, it meant there were spare copies in the library. She had one open on the table in front of her.

It wasn't making the essay any easier.

How thin is the line between laughter and tears!

There had been a woman who had fallen in love. She had left her husband and gone with her lover to the city of Troy. Her husband had followed with an army to attack the city. By the time the play started the war had been going on for ten years. And it went on going on, for scene after scene, with everybody being nasty and jealous, making speeches and then killing one another. First they killed each other bravely, and then they did it treacherously and cruelly. And when the curtain went down, the war was still going on. But you knew how it was going to end. Pretty well everybody would die. And the whole city would be destroyed.

Tick, tick, tick went the clock.

How thin is the line between laughter and tears?

Beneath that, her page was still blank. The first sentence was always the hardest. Once she'd got that down, then maybe she could get somewhere.

There's nothing to laugh about in Shakespeare's tragedies. Would that do?

Come to think about it, there wasn't much to laugh at in his so-called comedies either. Girl and boy run away together. Jilted boy goes after them.

Only, if it's a tragedy he takes an army with him.

Blank page. Somewhere down a corridor, someone shrieked. It might have been a happy noise. But it might not have been.

What choice did these people have? Things never worked the way they wanted. If it was tragedy, they were dead. If it was comedy, they were dopes. They were puppets on strings.

RRRRIIIIIINNGGGGG!

The clock had ticked all the way to half past. It was the end of break. Now it was hockey, with Miss Tackle. And Viola and Cassie and Imogen. And their sticks. Hurriedly and angrily, Sally's pen hit the page at last.

There's only one difference, she wrote. *In tragedy, our strings get cut.*

9: FIELD OF BATTLE

Tara looked into the dressing room. She tossed a green bib.

'Janey,' she said. 'You're with us.'

'Am I?' said Janey, catching it. 'If you say so.'

'You too, Ameena.'

'Hey!' said Billie. 'That's not fair!'

Janey and Ameena were the top sporty girls in Year Nine. They were both about six foot tall and competed at county level in tennis. Ameena also did long jump. Janey did showjumping to a level that Lolo could only dream of. And between them they represented the school in just about every sport, including a few unofficial ones. The King's Boys School still hadn't recovered from the day Janey had met up with them for some all-in arm wrestling.

'You'll have *six* team players on your side,' said Holly. 'And we haven't any!'

'Tough,' said Tara. She left. Janey followed her.

'Ameena – be a red. It's not fair.'

Ameena shrugged. She picked up the green bib.

'Ameena,' said Sally. 'We need a hand here.'

Ameena hesitated. She liked being paired with Janey. The two of them could criss-cross a ball through a defence like it was a needle through cloth.

But she was also the sort of person who would go out of her way for you, if you asked her right and didn't ask too much. She would for Sally, anyway.

'OK,' she said. 'I don't mind, I guess.'

'Right,' said Billie. 'Let's do it.' Her jaw jutted and she gripped her stick like a battle-axe. Whatever was coming, thought Sally, Billie was up for it. So was Holly. Tight-lipped, she strode out like a warrior. Ameena, head and shoulders above the rest of them, looked relaxed and confident. She wasn't part of this whole thing, anyway. Eva was playing goalie and was pretty well smothered in gloves and helmet and pads. But the others . . .

Sally touched Kaz on the arm. 'We're one too many now,' she said. 'Why don't you be our linesman?'

Kaz turned a pale face to her. 'Don't you want to be?'

'I managed to borrow some shin pads. But they're yours, if you want to play.'

'Lucky you! Well – thanks, but I'll go for the linesman option. Good luck!'

Miss Tackle was waiting for them on the field.

Miss Tackle!

She wasn't *really* wider than she was tall. She wasn't built of rough-cut oak either. She just looked that way.

Her hair was curly and cropped close. Her face was flat, her eyes were fierce. Out of doors she never spoke in anything less than a full bellow. She wore shorts in all weathers. She had probably never painted her fingernails in her entire life. She had, however, wrecked several rugby clubs.

She had a doctorate in Politics, played chess at regional level and was a mainstay of the school choir (in which she sang tenor). She was the darling of the school quiz team because she knew all the answers to everything, especially History. But competitive games were her passion. Deep in her fiery heart there was one unshakeable conviction – that even the meekest, most bespectacled and ill-coordinated student had a little Miss Tackle inside them somewhere, and the way to get it to come out was to chase them up and down the grass screaming and hitting everything you could. An hour on the pitch with Miss Tackle was an experience no one ever forgot. It was like meeting a mad-eyed, roaring tree stump that could move at astonishing speed.

'LINE UP, LADIES!' said Miss Tackle. 'LET'S GET STARTED!'

They got into their positions. Sally ran her eye over the field and her heart sank. The red team had Ameena and, well, Holly. The greens had Janey, as well as Viola, Cassie, Imogen and Tara, standing cold-eyed with their sticks in their hands. One thing about Viola and her friends – they might spend their days doing their nails and yawning about men, but they actually *could* play hockey. Times like this, you remembered that.

'HM, THIS ISN'T VERY EVEN, IS IT? VIOLA, WILL YOU SWAP WITH ELLIE PLEASE?'

'A masterstroke,' said Sally sourly, as an obviously reluctant Viola changed bibs with Ellie. 'Put her on our team, do.'

'Hey, Tony!' called Billie.

The sixth-formers were on a free period. There they went, lounging out of the school gates with their bags over their shoulders and their uniforms in studied disarray. Tony and Alec and Zac were trailing along in a threesome. They probably had no idea what was going on behind them.

'Hey Tony!' Billie called again, jumping up and down and waving her stick. She made enough noise for Tony to look her way. Worse, when he saw her he smiled and raised a hand. Everyone saw it. The faces of Viola and Cassie, Tara and Imogen, were as hard as stone. Their eyes glittered coldly.

'That does it,' muttered Sally. 'We're dead.'

Pheeeeeeeeep! went the whistle. *Clack, clack* went the sticks of the forwards and—

'Aargh!' cried Holly, hopping.

'Oh, sorry!' called Tara as she chased off after the ball.

'*Sorry,*' muttered Holly furiously. 'You will be!'

'You all right?' said Sally.

Holly rubbed her shin. 'She hit straight over it! Ow. I can walk. Let's get on.'

Down the field a cluster of red shirts was charging forward. Billie was there, stick clutched like a battle-axe and her fair hair bobbing as she ran. But Imogen

129

was on the ball first. Coolly and cruelly she waited until the eager reds had almost reached her, then she swept it aside to Tara, whose pass found Janey lancing up the field.

'TRACK BACK, REDS! WHO ARE YOU MARKING? LET'S SEE SOME DEFENCE NOW!'

Defence? The only defence against Janey was another Janey, and she didn't come in twos. Sally scampered after her, hoping for some kind of miracle that would let her get the ball. She might as well not have been there. Viola, sulking on the other wing, definitely wasn't there. Janey's pass found Tara in the centre with a free shot at goal, and only Eva, quivering behind her pads, in the way.

WHACK! went the stick. SMACK! went the ball, ricocheting off Eva's mask. 'Eeep!' said Eva, and sat down.

Tara pounced on the loose ball and drifted it contemptuously into the back of the red's net.

'GOAL! WELL DONE, TARA! COME ON, REDS, GET YOURSELVES ORGANIZED!'

'Are you all right?' said Sally. She had a horrible feeling she was going to be saying this a lot that afternoon.

'I – think – I – got a tooth or two left,' gasped Eva. She got to her feet. 'We're mincemeat, aren't we?'

There wasn't much Sally could say to that.

Here came the greens again. Janey – Tara – Imogen – Tara . . .

'COME ON, VIOLA, WHAT'S THE MATTER? ARE YOU ASLEEP?'

Viola broke into a sulky trot, arriving somewhere near Imogen just in time to see the ball crossed to the far side of the field. Tara picked it up. Sally was in the way. Back went Tara's stick . . .

WINDLEBERRY: The rules of hockey are perfectly clear. A player must not intimidate another player. They must not play the ball dangerously or in a way which leads to dangerous play. They may not intentionally raise the ball from a hit except for a shot at goal. Raising the ball towards another player within five metres is considered dangerous.

SALLY: You think any of that's going to stop her?

WINDLEBERRY: You should take the ball while her stick is back.

SALLY: *She isn't playing the ball!*

Sally could think very quickly. Quickly enough to jump back about two metres at the first sign of danger.

'Oh, *Sally!*' cried someone in despair.

Whisk! The ball had disappeared. Tara had disappeared. Where had she gone?

There! Right past her and racing for the goal!

WHACK!

Pheeeeeeep! Two–nil.

'Sorry, everybody,' mumbled Sally.

Five minutes later it was three.

'COME ON, REDS! DON'T DANCE AROUND LIKE TRIPPING FAIRIES! MAKE A GAME OF IT! GET THE BALL UPFIELD! COME ON! AMEENA'S ON HER OWN UP THERE!'

Another bully-off. This time Holly didn't even try for the ball. She flinched as Tara's stick came in, to howls from Miss Tackle and those one or two on her team who still thought there was any point in playing. Cassie was on it at once. She looked around. Janey was streaking up the middle, Tara and Imogen thundering down the right towards Sally.

Pass it up the middle, thought Sally. Up the middle, please . . .

Chock! It was coming almost straight for her.

So were Tara and Imogen. The pass was just a little long . . .

'GET ONTO IT, SALLY!' roared Miss Tackle.

'I'm going to have to,' groaned Sally. She stuck her stick out. The ball hit it, bounced away. She scrambled after it. Tara and Imogen were charging down on her like chariots with scythed wheels.

This is it! thought Sally. *I'm going to get hurt!*

She saw the ball spinning gently as it rolled away from her. She saw the blades of grass – the way that each one stood singly and cast its own shadow. She saw Kaz on the touchline, open-mouthed. She saw Ameena racing away down the field, looking back at her and pointing towards an open space as she ran . . .

Whack! went Sally's stick.

WHAM!

went everything else. The world went red. She had a sense of flying through the air, and then the field stood up and hit her all along her body. She couldn't see. She couldn't breathe.

'ADVANTAGE!' cried Miss Tackle happily. 'GOOD PASS, SALLY! GO ON, AMEENA, MAKE

SOMETHING OF IT! TACKLE HER, GREENS –
DON'T JUST STAND THERE! GO ON, AMEENA!
GO ON, AMEENA! YES, ALL THE WAY – GOAL!!!
THREE–ONE! BACK TO THE MIDDLE, LADIES,
LINE UP . . . !'

'Are you all right?' said a voice.

Is that me talking? thought Sally.

It wasn't. It was Kaz.

'Do you want to swap now?' she said hesitantly.

'I'm OK,' groaned Sally, and climbed slowly to her
feet. 'How much longer?'

'Just ten minutes, I think.'

Ten minutes. How many times could you get your
legs broken in ten minutes?

The players lined up. There was an air of fierce
triumph among the reds – the kind of dangerous,
angry joy that sweeps over the oppressed when they
finally put one back on their oppressors. Over the
greens – well, whatever it was, it was pretty fierce
too. Janey had said something to Tara and Imogen
and they were *not* pleased about it. White-faced,
mouths pursed, they squared up to their opponents.
Their sticks were held ominously close to waist
level.

Billie walked past Sally, with Eva and Holly at her

shoulder. 'We're going to *get* them!' she whispered fiercely.

What you're going to get, thought Sally, is Us All Killed.

Bully-off. Whack! '*Ow!*' cried Holly. '*Charge!*' cried Billie, and did. Off she went, haring down the field after the disappearing ball, with Eva and a pack of other reds at her shoulder. And they weren't taking prisoners either.

'Sticks!' shouted someone.

'PLAY ON!' cried Miss Tackle (who believed in the flow of the game). 'WELL DONE, IMOGEN, NOW GET IT UPFIELD! TRACK BACK, REDS, GET MARKING, LET'S SEE SOME DEFENCE . . . '

Here came the greens again – exactly as before. Imogen to Cassie, Cassie looking around, Janey speeding upfield, Tara bearing down on Sally at right back . . .

Holly was still crouching in the centre, clutching her shin. The play swept past her.

Whack! And here it came again, cruel, lethal, the little white ball spinning across the grass towards Sally with all the inevitability of death. Tara was chasing it like a hound. Desperately Sally tried to control it, scrabbling after it as it bounced away from her stick. Tara was beside her, poking for it. And up the field there was Ameena, exactly as before, running, pointing exactly as before . . .

Whack! went Sally's stick, and as it did so she tensed for the impact that would send her spinning into redness.

It didn't come. Tara sped away from her shouting, '*Mark Ameena! Stop her!*' Up the field Ameena gathered the ball. She had no support. Four green bibs were bearing down on her. On the far touchline Billie was shouting, 'Over here, Ameena! Over here!' She was in completely the wrong place.

Ameena wove. Click-clack went her stick and she was through them! The goal was ahead of her. So was Imogen.

'Go, Ameena, go!' yelled the reds.

'Stop her!' cried the greens.

'GET UP THERE, REDS! GIVE HER SOME SUPPORT! WHERE ARE YOU?!?'

Ameena seemed to hang in her stride. The defenders she had beaten were on her shoulder. Imogen was backing before her. She leaned one way, she went the other. She was away from them! She was through on goal!

'Stop her!' screamed Cassie.

'Stop her!' yelled Tara.

And Imogen, who was the only one who could do anything, did the only thing she could. Her stick sliced low through the air.

'*Aarghh!*' Ameena barked in pain and fell.

'Foul!' groaned the reds.

Pheeeeeeeep-pheeep! 'PENALTY HIT!' roared Miss Tackle. She dashed to the scene of the crime. Billie was ahead of her. Screaming '*Yaaaarrh!*' (or something like it) she pushed Imogen full in the chest and knocked her over. Angry cries broke from the greens. Tara caught Billie by the hair and yanked her head back.

'STOP!' bellowed Miss Tackle.

They stopped. There was an awful silence.

'Get off,' Miss Tackle said softly. 'The three of you. Wait for me on the touchline.'

Another time maybe they would have protested. ('But Miss *Tackle*! It wasn't *my* fault! *She* started it.' etc.) This time, no one did. They all knew it had gone too far. And when Miss Tackle spoke like that you did not argue. Billie strode to the touchline like a small ball of sparks. Tara and Imogen followed, coldly keeping their distance from her. No one said anything.

'Ameena?' said Miss Tackle.

Ameena did not get up. Her eyes were shut, her lips were drawn so the teeth showed. Shocked, the other girls gathered around her.

She's really hurt, thought Sally. Badly. And this wasn't anything to do with her. She wasn't taking sides. She was just playing for us because we asked her to.

Carefully, Miss Tackle began to unlace Ameena's boot.

'Holly's hurt too, Miss Tackle,' said someone.

Miss Tackle frowned at Holly, who had limped over to join them. 'Why aren't you wearing shin pads?' she said crossly.

'Someone took them, Miss Tackle,' said Holly.

Miss Tackle was still frowning. At a time like this, losing your kit was definitely your own fault.

'Can you walk?'

'Yes.'

'Go to the office and get it looked at.' She went back to unrolling Ameena's sock.

Ameena *had* been wearing shin pads, but it hadn't helped her. The edge of Imogen's stick had come slicing in just over the top of her boot and caught her full on the ankle. There was a vicious red mark there. It was already swelling. Miss Tackle tested it gently with her finger. Ameena sobbed.

138

'We need the stretcher,' said Miss Tackle.

The bell had gone for last period but Charlie B was still standing by the lockers illegally loading himself up from a packet of crisps.

Charlie was one of those boys who would one day discover weight training and turn himself into something surprisingly solid. But for the time being the gym was a bit distant, rather too much effort and a lot too expensive, and he got his exercise mostly by eating things he shouldn't. His big brother worked in a local takeaway, so some truly unbelievable stuff showed up in Charlie's packed lunches and none of it was ever less than a day old. Like most other Year Seven-to-Nine boys he lived in an entirely separate world, one ruled by anarchy and fantasy violence; but Sally had shown him how to multiply fractions last term and there remained between them some tenuous interplanetary contact.

'Here're your shin pads,' said Sally, handing them to him. 'Thanks.'

'Oh, right,' he said. 'Hope they helped.'

'I'm OK,' said Sally. 'But Ameena and Holly are both in the Accident Book, and Ameena's going to the hospital. Imogen and Tara and Billie are in front of the Deputy Head now.'

'That's tough. Did you know they've discovered an asteroid that might collide with the Earth in a few months? They've called it Zebukun.'

This was the sort of news that Charlie genuinely thought could cheer people up.

'. . . I reckon if it hits in our hemisphere we're bound to see something. That'd be so cool!'

'If you say so. By the way . . .'

'Umm?'

'Where *did* Billie get that mouse?'

'Why ask me?' said Charlie, showing no surprise.

'I just thought – if I had to find a dead mouse in school, whose pockets would I search first?'

'You can search 'em now,' said Charlie innocently.

'What would I find if I did?'

Charlie smiled a tight little smile.

'Stay out of it, Charlie. It only makes things worse.'

'You know what I'm going to be when I grow up? I'm going to be a gun-runner. Rich'll be pushing smack but I'll be running guns, dodging patrols, breaking blockades, all that. Guns are cool.'

'You,' said Sally, 'are going to be a chemist. Rich will be an engineer. And you'll each have a wife and two kids and you'll be very proud . . .'

'Don't *say* that!'

'But if you see Tony Hicks?'

'Yeah?'

'You could drop a toad down his trousers for me . . .'

WINDLEBERRY: Sally!

'. . . Preferably one of the poisonous type.'

It took a moment for her words to filter across whatever light-years divided Charlie's personal universe from reality. Then, slowly, a kind of light began to grow in his eyes. Deep within his brain thoughts fired and ideas came wheeling into focus. Mental capacities that were kept firmly shut down for 90% of the school day soared to full power. A smile spread over his lips, as if he were an artist who had glimpsed in some clouded sunset a gleam of the walls of Heaven.

'Could get him to swallow a frog. How about it?'

WINDLEBERRY: *Sally!*

'Forget it,' sighed Sally. 'I was only joking. Thanks for the shin pads, anyway. You really saved my life.'

'Y'r welcome.'

10: THE ANGEL OF LOVE

It is time to consider the sex of an angel.

Angels have no sex. They don't need one. An angel is an 'it' rather than a 'he' or a 'she'. This is true even if – like the cupids – their physical appearance very strongly suggests something else.

Angels can appear as anything. It could be a shaft of light or a wonderful smell, or a voice speaking from the air. Traditionally, however, they appear as a person. And again traditionally, that person is almost always male.

Why?

Probably it's because when angels appear it's to hand out orders, and Tradition has always found it easier to take orders from men. It's something to do with the deeper voice, the bushier eyebrows and the hint that you'll get beaten up if you don't do as you're told. There's no point getting upset about this. That's the way Tradition is. Or was.

So angels mostly appear as 'he' and are mostly referred to as 'he'.

There is one angel, however, who has very good reasons for appearing as 'she' at least half the time, and has spent her career operating almost exclusively as 'she' under names such as Venus, Aphrodite, Aidin, Branwen, Chalchiuhtlicue, Erzulie, Hathor and so on. It is she who lights the divine passion in the heart of human souls. It is she who commands the cupids. She is the Angel of Love and her seat is in a chamber in one of the highest towers of Heaven.

Now, suppose that it were possible to enter that chamber (without melting). Suppose that your eyes were to adjust to the glare and the glory, that you looked around. What would you see?

All right, the Mirrors of Burning Glances, the Arch of Pure Joy, yes, yes. But what else? You know you can get clues about a person if you're in a room they use a lot. What *else* would you see?

Would you, possibly, see that the Chamber of Glory was . . .

. . . maybe . . .

. . . just a little untidy?

Like, these *piles* of letters and reports and things everywhere?

Love is patient. Love is kind. She does not envy, she does not boast, she is not proud. She is not rude, she is not self-seeking, she is not easily angered, she keeps no record of wrongs. In fact, she prefers to keep no records of any kind at all. Love is just ♥ ♥ ♥ ♥ when it comes to paperwork.

The paper streams in through the door, with lots of things written on it that people think Love ought to see or know or do something about. And then it gets added to the piles. Which pile? Take your pick – it doesn't matter. Usually her secretary adds it to whichever one is lowest and least likely to collapse under its own weight. So they rise and rise – amazing, teetering constructions, until they appear more like a model of some great city on a hill than the workload of an important angel assembled on an important angel's desk.

Oh, yes. About that desk . . .

There had been a woman who had begged that her heart should live on after her death, so that she might love her lover from beyond the grave.

'Sure,' the angel had said. She liked this sort of thing.

'There you go,' she had said, a moment later. 'Now, er, what shall I do with it?'

So she was using it as her desk.

This wasn't as good an idea as it seemed at the time. A living heart has no flat surfaces, is a bit sticky and tends to move up and down rather a lot. The moving up and down isn't immediately obvious when it's hidden under the forest of marking, reports, files, letters, memos, test papers and coursework, the indefinite storage of which is what this angel thinks a desk is for. But it's there beneath it all, valiantly labouring on, loving its lost lover. Occasionally the weight of bureaucracy is just too much and it has a seizure, whereupon the angel has to resuscitate it by thumping it as hard as she can with her fist. But she's the sort of angel who thumps her desk from time to time anyway so there's usually no problem about this.

On it beats, on and on, although the woman and her lover both passed the gates of Death long ago. And the towers of paper shake and shift gently with each pulse, and every now and then another pile of marking sidles to the point where the not-very-flat surface becomes a not-very-straight side, and there it gives one last teeter, a slight wail, and tumbles and spills all across the Tiles of Willing Sacrifice until it comes to rest at last against the Wall of Desire, or against the foot of a full-length Mirror of Burning Glances (whereupon it starts to smoulder). That might have bothered another angel, but not this one.

It's not that she doesn't focus on things. She just focuses differently. She has an instant, total kind of focus where suddenly the only thing in the world or the universe that matters at all is whether someone called Jules will look round and see someone called Sarah watching from the crowd. Zoom, and she's there! The eyes lock, the pulses bounce, the rest of the room goes blurry and it's job done. Love can do this a million times in an hour, although generally she doesn't work at that rate because it takes a few seconds for the heart to cook properly and she thinks it's better not to rush it.

She once shocked the entire Celestial Staff Room by suggesting that every angel in Heaven should have their own computer. This was not because she wanted to catch up on her paperwork. It was because she had heard about online dating and reckoned that if the rest of her market was going digital then so should she. Heaven, she told her colleagues, should move with the times.

(The Staff rather struggled with the concept of

'times'. The Choirmasters asked if she meant 3/4 time, 4/4 time, 5/8 time or something sort of jazzy. The Appeals Board never even got as far as 'times' because they were still struggling with the word 'move'. This is pretty much what happens every time she comes up with an idea. Deep down, Love is one really frustrated little archangel.)

More facts about Love:

1) She likes being a woman;
2) She likes giving orders;
3) She *doesn't* like Tradition. Tradition goes around in whalebone corsets and an ankle-length dress, insisting that everything be arranged through the parents, preferably with a bride-price and while the couple are still too young to think of thinking for themselves.

In a place like Heaven, it's always going to be an uphill battle for her. Even her own cupids prefer to think of 'her' as a 'he'. Somehow they just felt that life as a cupid is tough enough what with being short, fat, naked et cetera, without having to take orders from a girl as well. They like to see her in one of her male forms, such as Eros, the winged archer, the God of Passion. As Eros, she is as close as she ever comes to being a cupid herself. That is, she is about the same weight and only several times the height.

Not that they *call* her 'Eros'. No way. They are cupids. They call her 'boss'. Or sometimes 'Dirty Erry'.

As in . . .

'Yer've visitors, Erry,' said her secretary.

'Visitors?' says the angel, in tones of honeyed surprise. 'Am I expecting anyone?'

She is not expecting anyone. And since it is her secretary's job to be expecting anyone or anything that she isn't expecting so that he can tell her in time for her to expect it, and he hadn't, everything is his fault. This comes as no surprise to the cupid, who learned on his first day that '*Everything is your fault*' is his job description in four words.

'They're 'ere anyways, Erry.'

'Then you must show them in, my darling, mustn't you?'

She knew who it was. She felt his approach before he entered, like the pull of gravity from a huge dark star. She felt the billions of years, the slowness, the patience, the coldness of death, the inevitability of ending. She felt him coming closer. She rose to her feet.

148

Love met Doom in the chambers of Heaven.

They were two ancient creatures. She was warmth and a great light, he emptiness and everlasting cold. Both were massive in their knowledge and power and understanding. There were few secrets of Creation that one or other of them did not know. In a moment of depth and silence, they bowed.

The moment was interrupted by Mishamh, who stepped between them with his feathers all fluffed like a robin about to fight. 'We have come,' he announced, 'to warn you that we are raising a complaint with the Governors about the Department of Love.'

Love blinked at him. 'You're so sweet,' she said.

Complaining to the Governors was the Heavenly equivalent of sending in the tanks. *'You're so sweet,'* was not the answer Mishamh had expected.

'The Department of Love is obstructing the work of the Appeals Board!' he said sternly.

'Aw, shucks!' said Love.

'The Department of Love,' declared Mishamh, 'has for THIRTY CENTURIES frustrated EVERY date and deadline for the End of the World that has EVER been decreed!'

'☹' said Love.

'As detailed in our list of charges.' The young angel

149

held out a scroll written in letters of meteorite trail upon the stuff of adamant, which is what the Physics staff tend to use when they are upset.

'We assume you will provide us with a copy of your response,' said Mishamh haughtily.

Love smiled. A scroll of moonlight appeared in her long fingers, inscribed with the notes of a nightingale's song. She blew it as if it were a kiss towards the dark figure of Doomsday. He read it. His mouth twitched, a little.

Mishamh looked to his master.

'She requests that you be transferred to her department,' he said. 'As soon as your duties allow.'

'*What?!?*'

'He's just so handsome when he's angry,' said the Angel of Love.

'But . . . our Complaint . . .' stammered Mishamh.

Before his eyes the Angel of Love tossed the charge sheet of adamant carelessly into the air. At once it became a cloud of sparkling dust, from which troops of little cupids seemed to fly with mocking, silvery laughter to circle around his head. Every one of those little naked creatures was himself.

The room seemed to be spinning. The desk at which the angel stood was definitely going up and down, which didn't help matters at all.

He heard Doomsday say, 'I fear my subordinate is engaged on a project of considerable importance.'

'Which will soon be considerably *un*important, I believe,' said Love. 'At least for the next two thousand six hundred years. You could apply for him to be transferred back once your asteroid was on its way in again, couldn't you?'

'I could . . .'

'But . . . the Great Curriculum!' cried Mishamh. 'We're making a mockery of everything it says! We *have* to destroy the world!'

'What, all of it?' said the Angel of Love.

'All of it,' said Mishamh, rallying as best he could. 'Every last living thing. The earth they stand on. The air they breathe . . .'

'The children? The little furry animals?'

'Yes, all.'

'Isn't that rather – sad?'

'Sad?'

'*I* think it's sad.'

'It is indeed sad,' said Doomsday. 'And it is Right. Sorrow is a part of the Curriculum. For a time.'

'The Governors want it to happen!' said Mishamh.

'Are you sure of that?' said Love.

'Of course I'm sure!'

'Maybe they like little furry animals . . .'

'The Governors have said "All must be made Perfect,"' Mishamh cried. 'If a thing cannot be made perfect, then it must not be. That means the Earth *must* be destroyed. The deadlines for destruction are set by the Governors themselves. *Why* won't you let it happen?'

There was a moment of shocked silence. It seemed to spread out far beyond the room, beyond the towers of Love. It rolled down the corridors and galleries of Heaven like an icy chill, and hidden within its shivering heart was that whisper: *Why?*

It was felt everywhere. Souls were distracted from their lessons. Choirs faltered, sentinels looked over their shoulders. The Governors, meeting in committee, ruffled their papers uncomfortably. Behind the doors of the Head's study, something stirred and sighed.

'Ah,' said Doomsday.

'Oh,' said the Angel of Love.

'I'm sure my colleague didn't mean . . .'

'I'm *sure* he didn't,' said the angel sweetly.

' . . . to use that word,' Doomsday finished. 'Of

course, Love is also part of the Curriculum. It is ordained by the Governors, who are the source of all order in Heaven. We understand that. We do not question it . . .'

'I'm so glad . . .'

'. . . in quite the way that my colleague may have implied. Nevertheless' – the angel raised a dangerous eyebrow – 'nevertheless, my colleague – whom I am afraid cannot be immediately released from my department – makes a number of points that seem apt. Simply put, that the Great Curriculum moves with the Laws of Heaven. The Laws of Heaven point to the ending of the world. This conclusion is inescapable. Creation has no meaning if there is not also Destruction. Perfection cannot be perfected if it is shackled to Imperfection. Yet, because of the actions of your servants at the Appeals Board, the Destruction of Imperfection continues to be postponed.'

'You've said this before, you know.'

'I have. I note, however, that this time you have not denied that it is your servants who are responsible for the delay.'

'Dear me! Did I say they were?'

'According to the Great Curriculum, the world must end,' Doomsday went on mildly. 'Therefore the

Appeal will one day be decided. At that point, the very large number of additional souls who have been born since the first deadline was postponed (most of whom are still waiting in the Gallery of Penitence, the Stair of Sincerity and the Hall of Lamentation) will have to start their classes. And since most have appealed on some ground or other connected with the subject of Love, one may imagine that Love will feature heavily on their timetable.'

He paused, as if waiting for an answer. The angel made none.

'You will be busy, I think,' Doomsday concluded. 'Dear me, yes. I do not know if you are looking forward to this. But I certainly am.'

Another silence, colder by several degrees than the last. The two great angels bowed once again to each other. Then Doomsday left, with his young assistant trailing in his wake. Love watched them go.

'Silly old fool,' she muttered.

She said it, but she felt less serene than an angel should. Doomsday was neither silly nor foolish. He had existed for billions of years longer than she, since the days when Heaven had been a much emptier place with only the Head, a few Governors and a handful of wild-eyed astronomers to get things started. He was patient. He was calculating. He was saying that in the end the Governors would be forced by their own laws to side with him. And if he was right, then yes, there would be a terrible amount of clearing up to do.

But was he?

Love knew quite well that she and her cupids had been upsetting Heaven's Appeals process for three thousand years. *That* didn't bother her. She also knew the answer to Mishamh's question 'Why?'

It was because she was Love. Just that.

Love couldn't be put in a box. Certainly not in a witness box. It couldn't be made part of a process. It must keep bursting out, getting in the way, turning black into white and white into all the colours of the rainbow. This was what Love was. It simply wasn't in her nature to do things any other way.

> Key Fact: Love = Chaos

Love made things happen when everything else said they shouldn't. Love broke rules because they were there to be broken. Yet she too was a part of Heaven.

And if a thing was, in Heaven, then it was as it should be. If you asked Love to your Appeal, and your Appeal got tied up in knots because of it, then that too was as it should be.

One day, maybe soon, or maybe many thousands of years away, the Governors would have to choose between Love and Doom. Not even Love knew what they would do, or when it would be.

The one thing she did know was anyone who thought *she* was going to clear all of this up would be sorely mistaken. Clearing up was what happened to other people.

Among the piles on her desk there was a small bell. It sat there tinging gently each time the heart beat. She lifted a golden hammer and struck it.

'Yes, Erry?' said her secretary hoarsely, from the outer room.

'Who's handling the Appeal for us now?'

The cupid checked the back of his hand, which like bad kids everywhere he used as a notebook.

'It's Spikey. You said he needed a break from fieldwork.'

'Did I? I suppose I did. Ask Spikey to step in to see me. It's time we changed tactics.'

A plan was forming in Love's mind. A very, very

Loving plan. The sort that burned cities.

'He will need something rather special. From our, er, weapons people. You'll be a darling and do the paperwork for me, won't you?'

A sulky mumble from the other room. Cupids didn't like paperwork any more than Love herself. Love ignored it. Her thoughts had shifted on to something else. Speaking of cities . . .

This whole Appeal thing hadn't come out of nowhere. It had been started by someone. As far as Love was concerned, that someone was unfinished business.

'By the way – I'm expecting a complaint, about a Miss Jones of Darlington Row. Hasn't it arrived yet?'

The secretary suppressed a groan. 'I'll come and find it for yer, Erry.'

Love stood thoughtfully to one side while he appeared and started searching through the piles on her desk with a pitchfork.

She never made promises. Not the sort she had to keep. In Love, lots of things got said and lots of good intentions got intended. But they weren't contracts. You could walk away from them if you wanted to. That was the whole point. Cupids could drop pink hearts in people's minds to say 'essential maintenance will be carried out here'. That was all right. They could attach pink hearts to their arrows to say 'we apologize for any inconvenience'. That was accepted.

But they never, ever, EVER attached notes to say 'If you are not completely satisfied with our service . . .'

That is, no cupid would ever, ever, EVER do it again.

Love is not easily angered . . .

(Such a giveaway, that word 'easily' . . .)

Love keeps no record of wrongs . . .

The angel had no need to keep a record. The 'fifty-page incident' was not exactly something she was being allowed to forget. Nor had she forgotten who caused it. She had approved his transfer out of her department immediately. And since then she had remembered him. At least, she had remembered him often enough to keep remembering. With her peculiar and erratic focus, she had been waiting through the centuries.

For the day he became a Guardian.

(The polite way to describe the relationship between cupids and guardian angels is this: You could never get them to sing off the same sheet, you could never get them to sing in unison, and you would *really* have to stretch your definition of 'harmony'. All this was said by an Angelic Choirmaster who had actually tried.)

Cupids and Guardians both did what most other angels didn't do. They went down to Earth and worked with what they found there, i.e. humans and all the things that were wrong with them. This did NOT mean they were allies. Two thirds of all that paper on the desk of Love came from unhappy guardian angels who were having to live with what the cupids had done to their human after the cupids had packed up and moved on to the next job.

And the Guardians wanted the Angel of Love to know about it. *You didn't ought to have done it,* they wrote (in angel-speak). *My human is out of control. Danger to themselves and everyone around them. Sleepless nights. Suicidal thoughts. Overload – overload* etc.

My darling Windleberry. Do you know how much trouble you have caused me?

Maybe you do.

Can you guess, then, what I'm about to put you through?

Perhaps you're thinking: *All right. A few nights without sleep won't kill us. A few weeks of pining we can deal with . . .*

You have no idea what you are in for. You have no idea – yet.

'Got it, Erry,' said her sweating cupid at last. He heaved it out from under a thousand other reports that had come in the same morning.

'Thank you. You're a sweetie.'

A thousand reports – but this was the one for which she had waited through thirty centuries. She had already had the Objection he sent. It had arrived almost immediately after the pink heart had been delivered. But the Objection wasn't the same as the heartfelt cry of Protest, the anguish of someone who was a slave to Order, finding that his life was now to be ruled by Chaos.

And here it was: *Miss Jones of Darlington Row. Formal Complaint.*

Lovely.

Lovely, my dear Windleberry. I'm going to enjoy your little essay. I hope you've written it with feeling. I think I might frame it.

I'm going to enjoy the next one too. And the next . . .

Slowly, smiling, she opened the cover. The Heading read:

Formal Protest
to the Department of Love

Re: Miss B Jones of Darlington Row . . .

She frowned. Miss *B* Jones? That wasn't the initial she was expecting.

She turned straight to the end of the report.

The signature wasn't the one she had expected either.

'FUG!'

11: GHOST

Billie was in detention. She spent it writing a love letter to Tony. She hadn't decided if she was actually going to give it to him. What she wanted was for him to notice her without her seeming to try. But Imogen and Tara were in the same detention and Billie knew that it would make them mad.

Imogen and Tara also spent their detention writing letters. They were poison pen letters, to Billie.

Sally went home and told Mum that there was going to be a call from school about Billie. Mum took paracetamol and went to lie down.

Somewhere halfway through Sally's R.E. essay, her phone buzzed. It was a text from Ameena, replying to one Sally had sent her earlier.

No bones brokn thank God but ill mis match next wk.

V soz 2 hear, Sally thumbed back. Bud Luk. She put the phone down and picked up the dictionary. The phone buzzed again.

Ill live. Woz gud pas. U shd be in team.

'Aargh, the curse of Miss Tackle!' muttered Sally. No thx I like this life, she sent back.

2 bad. They'll need players. Have taken out contract on Immy.

Tight-lipped, Sally put the phone down. She picked up her pen. She tried to think about comparisons between Sikhism and Islam. She found she couldn't. She put her pen down and picked up her phone again.

nt her fault, she texted. Stuf goin on.

'Not that that changes anything,' she said, as she put her phone down again.

It didn't.

> 2 bad 4 her she dint have 2 cripple me.
> Assasins closng in.

The passages of Sally's mind were dark. The air within them was heavy, as if a small thunderstorm was brooding somewhere. Her thoughts chased through them fretfully. They had no power.

'Imogen only did it because of Viola,' she said. 'And Ameena was only playing for us because I asked her to. And now someone else is going to get dragged in, because of what Imogen did to Ameena! It'll probably be Janey. Janey's *nice*!'

Walk, walk, walk, through the corridors of crystal where everything was in its place and nothing met her need. The monuments and images looked down and could not speak. The words on the walls had no meaning. Windleberry strode beside her, head bowed. This air of grief and anger was like acid to him. There was nothing he could do about it. He could only endure it. He was patient, powerless, everlasting. He stayed with her.

'We should just let Viola and Billie sort it out between them. Mud pies at ten paces. Or maybe teeth and nails.'

'That wouldn't solve anything,' said Windleberry.

'It would keep *us* out of it.'

'And what does it do for Viola and Billie?'

'But it's their fault! It's Billie's fault, anyway. Why did she have to set herself at Tony?'

'Is that why you're angry with her?'

(Walk, walk, walk, in the darkness of the thoughts of her mind.)

'No,' said Sally. 'All right – it's because she got him to notice her. Why her? Except that she did it by shouting and screaming.'

'She didn't scream.'

'No, maybe not. But she did shout. Twice.'

'And if it had been you he had noticed,' said Windleberry, 'wouldn't you have wanted Billie and the others to back you up?'

'You sound just like my dad sometimes.'

'You know why that is, don't you?'

'Don't go there,' growled Sally.

Behind them, slumped and forlorn, trailed Muddlespot. He knew he should be at Sally's other shoulder, putting lots of ideas and cunning plans to her that would have all sorts of interesting consequences. His bosses down in Low Command had written whole books on situations like these – big black-bound books with pages of human skin. If they found out what was happening here he would be bombarded with instructions and suggestions. Probably more than he could read, let alone carry out. Maybe they'd even send a team of consultants! He shuddered.

His heart wasn't in it. His life was misery. He felt physically sick. He could not take his eyes off Windleberry, and yet he knew that he was the one thing that Windleberry most hated, despised and thought lower than dirt. Being with him was agony. Being without him was emptiness.

'I don't think Tony really cares about either of them!' said Sally.

'I feel their pain,' sighed Muddlespot.

'*SHUT UP!*' said both Sally and Windleberry.

'Sorry,' he mumbled.

'If only Billie would fall for someone else, maybe it'll all start to die down. But what's the chance of that?'

'None,' said Muddlespot. 'Take it from me. No chance. Whatsoever.'

They turned and looked at him then. He folded his arms and fixed Windleberry with a defiant stare.

A thoughtful expression crossed Windleberry's face. One square finger stroked the point of his square jaw.

'Another golden arrow, another boy for Billie?' snarled Muddlespot. 'Is that what you're thinking?'

'Maybe. Why not?'

'Listen. I've been on the sharp end of one of these things. I know. There's no way you can change what they do!'

'In some cases – a few – you are right.' Windleberry was still looking thoughtfully at Muddlespot. 'Even so, there *is* a chance.'

'Do tell!'

'The golden arrow causes the victim to fall in love. But for some very rare, very special cases, the cupids have another arrow. A leaden one. It has the opposite effect.'

'Can you get it? asked Sally.

'I know where it is kept. I know how to use it. What I need is an idea.'

'I'm full of ideas,' said Sally. 'Ideas are what I do. Big ones, small ones, made to order – exactly what kind of idea did you want?'

'I need an idea,' said Windleberry, 'of flesh-coloured paint.'

He weighed up Muddlespot with his eye.

'I should say three buckets of it. At least.'

12: TAKE ME TO HEAVEN

Sally dreamed that she was under the night sky. Someone was sitting beside her. She liked him being there. She could rest her head on his shoulder and look up at the stars. They were brilliant – thousands and thousands of tiny points of white fire. One slid from its place and flashed across the sky, drawing a streak of light behind it, growing and growing even as she watched.

'What's that?' she said to the boy beside her.

'Death,' he answered as he took her hand.

She woke and looked at the darkness. There were no stars, and no one was with her (unless she counted Shades, who had somehow found his way through her firmly-shut door so that he could curl up on her pillow and sneeze into her ear in the small hours).

She felt wide awake, and yet somehow not awake enough to get up and throw Shades out again.

She thought about an asteroid hitting the Earth. That would not be cool. Lots of people might die. Maybe everyone would.

She thought about all the things she wanted to do and wouldn't be able to if it happened. Suddenly she wasn't sure if she had got the right ones, anyway.

She wondered who the voice in her dream had been, and whether it had been Zac Stenton. Zac wasn't just good to look at. He noticed you. He was worth two Alecs and three Tonys, because of the way he'd grin and lift his eyebrow at you as you passed in the corridor. And that gig he had done at the end-of-term assembly had been side-splitting.

She wondered how long she was going to have to lie here before morning.

Then suddenly it *was* morning, and her alarm was beating out Cindy Platter's *I Love Ya Real*. So she must have slept again. She forced herself up, got dressed in a daze and made her bed as she always did. She could hear the family moving around the house. Mum was knocking on Billie's door.

Downstairs for breakfast. Greg, unshaven, was trying to talk to Mum. Mum wasn't answering –

something was wrong between them again. No good asking what. One side of Sally's toast was black and brown, the other practically raw. The toaster had been on its last legs for months. She ate it, anyway. She tried to decide, again, what Marmite really tasted of. She tried not to think what was going to happen at school.

Mum knocked on Billie's door for the second time. If she had to do it again she would shout. Greg slurped his coffee. That was one of the things that Mum hated, but somehow he couldn't stop doing it. One day, soon, something was going to go snap between them. As if there wasn't enough going on already.

Billie was up – unusual that she had managed it before Mum started shouting. She had gone straight into the bathroom, just as Sally was clearing her plate and was ready to go upstairs. Why couldn't she have come down to get breakfast? But no, she was in the bathroom, and now no one else could get in there until she had finished.

Sally's bag was packed. She had done that the evening before – R.E. books, Maths and History, as well as the English for Mr Kingsley. Her games clothes had dried overnight. She folded them and put them in her sports bag. There were no bloodstains on any of them, which was astonishing. Billie's kit was still hanging on the radiator. It looked as if one of Billie's sports socks had got lost somewhere in the washing process. Probably it had never made it into the machine in the first place. Mum-and-Billie screaming match, here we come. *When* Billie managed to get out of the bathroom.

'Right,' grumbled Greg, passing in the hall below. 'I'm off. Maybe someone at the office will be pleased to see me.'

The front door closed behind him.

She'd be more pleased to see you, thought Sally, if you could be the same for her.

Here came Mum, climbing the stairs. 'Isn't Billie up? I thought I heard her?'

'She's up all right,' said Sally. 'She just can't get past the mirror.'

Mum looked at the bathroom door in surprise. She banged on it.

'In a minute,' came Billie's voice.

'What's she doing?' said Mum.

'Her make-up, at a guess.'

'*Billie's* doing make-up?'

You haven't spotted a thing, have you? thought Sally. Amazing what grown-ups don't notice.

'But Billie never makes up!' said Mum.

She was this morning. She was making up thoroughly and carefully. And breakfast, sports kit, schoolbags, the whole of the rest of the world, could just wait until she was finished.

Mum banged on the door again. 'Billie?'

'In a *minute*, I said.'

'It's just that we're all waiting out here!'

She had got to the bathroom ten minutes early, Sally calculated. How long could she take over a five-minute job? Fifteen minutes? Twenty? It was ten to eight already.

'I'll wash my face in the kitchen,' she said. Make-up would have to wait till she got a moment at school. Teeth, until she got back home again. She'd have all day to decide what Marmite tasted like now. Joy.

'Billie!' Thump-thump-thump.

'All *right*! Billie catapulted from the bathroom. At the top of the stairs she looked herself over in the mirror, sideways. Sally saw her frown as she took in the profile (or lack of it) of her chest. Why couldn't you have a film star's body parts when you needed them? Too bad, Billie. Find some other way to pull your boy. Preferably without getting the rest of us murdered.

She hadn't done a bad job on her face, though.

She really meant business today.

'Keep still,' said Windleberry. With a fine brush he dabbed at Muddlespot's cheek. Once.

'What was that?' said Muddlespot.

'A dimple,' Windleberry said. 'At least, that's what it will look like.'

The Inner Sally passed, dressed for school and wiping at her face with a kitchen towel. She glanced at them and frowned. 'Are you sure that will work?'

'Of course I'm sure,' said Windleberry. 'Why shouldn't it?'

Because, Muddlespot thought, I am standing in a coat of flesh-coloured paint. *Thick* flesh-coloured paint. I smell of flesh-coloured paint, I drip flesh-coloured paint, I even sweat flesh-coloured paint. When I move, I'm going to leave flesh-coloured footprints wherever I go. And if I wait till it dries, it'll start to crack and peel and I'll look like a walking encyclopedia of flesh-coloured skin diseases.

'Just have faith,' said Windleberry.

It was possible, Muddlespot discovered, to be both madly in love with someone and yet to have no faith in them at all.

'This is. *Not*. Going to work,' he said.

'Yes it is,' said Windleberry. 'Wig.' He plonked a wig of soft blond curls on Muddlespot's head.

'How can you be sure?'

'I know them. You don't.'

'Yeah? And how much do you know, exactly?'

'I was one of them once,' said Windleberry grimly.

Muddlespot staggered. He tried to imagine Windleberry in the wayward chubbiness of a cupid's body. He couldn't do it. Everything about his hero was neat, crisp, straight lines. The jacket, the bow tie, the squareness of his jaw, the littleness of his mouth, even the cut of his fiery hair. He was a dream of geometry, a mass of powerful rectangles and triangles. His circumference at the shoulder was approximately twice that of his waist, and both were trim.

'*You* were a cupid?'

'I'm surprised too,' said Sally.

'The day I left them, I went and locked myself in the Celestial Gym for a hundred years,' said Windleberry. 'By the time I walked out, no one recognized me.'

'I bet they didn't.' said Sally, open-mouthed. 'You pumped iron for *a hundred years*?'

'Iron? No. I started on White Dwarfs and worked up to Black Holes.'

'That's gotta hurt!'

'The pain did not matter,' said Windleberry grimly. 'All it means for us now is that I haven't the shape to pass for a cupid. And *he* has.' He jerked a thumb, square and powerful, at the hapless Muddlespot.

'Some of it anyway,' he added.

'You'll have to do something about his tail,' said Sally.

'I'm going to. Stay still . . .' He bent down.

'What are you . . . Ow!' cried Muddlespot. 'Hey! My tail is part of me! I demand that you show it resp— *Ow!* What are you *doing?*'

'All done,' said Windleberry, rising.

'What did you . . . ?' said Muddlespot pitifully. He looked down.

It felt as if his tail – his beautiful, long, hairy-tipped tail, which was the pride of any self-respecting demon – had been dragged between his legs, looped once around each thigh and then tied in a tight little bow between his legs with only the tip poking out.

That was what it *felt* like. He couldn't actually see it, because his tummy was in the way.

Sally could.

'Well,' she said at last. 'It's in the right place, and it's in *roughly* the right shape. But do you really think he'll get away with it?'

'They won't give it a second glance,' said Windleberry.

'How can you be sure?'

'They'll all be averting their eyes.'

It was half a mile from the Jones house to the gates of Darlington High. It *could* be done in five minutes. If they ran.

Aching, sweating, gasping, Sally and Billie pounded into the playground. The bell had gone. The clamour was dying in the classrooms and corridors. Registration was beginning. If you weren't in your place when your name was called, you got a 'Late'. Last year Billie had clocked up thirty-four 'Lates' in two and a half terms, which was a school record. After that Mum had made her rule about the twins leaving the house together, since when Billie had been on time (just about) every morning and both girls were a lot fitter than they otherwise would have been.

Half a mile, with a ton of books and a sack of PE kit. *You* try it sometime.

They had made it, just. The last pupils were still hurrying down the corridors. Charlie B was still leaning by the lockers, finishing his breakfast (a kebab of some kind). Sally and Billie slung their P.E. bags onto the top of their lockers and scuttled for the classroom door.

Wham! The way was blocked by a wall of school uniforms. Quite a high wall too. Cassie, Viola and Imogen weren't really twice as tall as the twins, but this morning they looked it.

'All right,' said Cassie. 'Where is it?'

The twins looked up at them.

'Imogen's oboe,' said Cassie. 'Where have you put it?'

'Put it?'

'It was there last night,' said Cassie. 'It's gone this morning. Someone's taken it. And who might that have been?'

'Must have been whoever took the shin pads yesterday,' growled Billie.

'That is *not* funny,' said Cassie.

There was an air of cold fury about Cassie and Viola that was worse, if anything, than the very worst they had looked the day before. Imogen was glaring like the others, but there was something trembly about her glare that made it look as if she was about to burst into tears. She was a shade paler than she should have been.

Stealing boyfriends was one thing, their looks said.

Putting dead mice in a girl's bag, OK. But walk off with an oboe . . .

'She's got her Grade Five this afternoon,' said Cassie. 'I suppose you'll tell us you didn't know.'

'Oh,' said Sally.

Oh.

How do you get at a girl you really want to hurt? Pick something that matters and spoil it. Nothing mattered as much in Imogen's family as music. They spent hours at it. She and her brothers were ticking off their exams one after the other. Grade 4, Grade 5, Grade 6. There'd be a Music Diploma too, at some point, But the thing about exams was, you don't just have to be good at it. You have to be in the right place, and the right time. With your music. And your instrument.

Ameena had been right. The assassins had closed in.

'It wasn't us,' said Sally. 'We've just got here.'

The three looked down at the twins. At their flushed faces, heavy breathing, shirts that had come untucked during the run from home. It was obvious that she was telling the truth.

'We'll all get "Lates", standing around like this,' Sally pleaded.

'Then let's do that, shall we?' said Cassie.

'We'll say we were looking for the oboe,' said Viola. 'And *you* were helping us.'

'I can't do it!' cried Muddlespot.

'Yes you can,' said Windleberry.

'Just go!' urged the Inner Sally. 'Things are getting really bad out there!'

'*You don't understand!*'

They stared at him.

'Look at me!' Muddlespot cried.

'We are,' said Sally.

'I mean – *I* can't go to Heaven. *He* can. Maybe you can. But not *me*! I'm everything that place isn't. I'm – I'm deceit. I'm foul. I'm pride – and proud of it. I can't *begin* to get there! And if I did, it'd kill me, just being there. Anyway, the Fluffies will tear me to pieces!'

Windleberry looked thoughtful.

'How do you think I'm going to do it?' Muddlespot pleaded.

Still Windleberry looked thoughtful.

'There's a song,' Sally said, 'that Mum sings in the shower – *Three Steps To Heaven*. Step One, you find a boy to love. Step Two, he falls in love with—'

'That won't be necessary,' said Windleberry. 'Muddlespot,' he said. 'Follow me.'

Muddlespot teetered on his toes. It was the first time that Windleberry (his beloved and admired Windleberry!) had ever spoken his name. The sound of it shook him to his core. It hauled him forwards. Even as every ounce of his own being hauled him back.

'Follow me,' said Windleberry. He seemed to be climbing a set of stairs – stairs that had somehow appeared in Sally's mind. They were ordinary, straight stairs. No gold, no marble, no statues or ornate carvings. Just very, very plain, drudging steps, and each one was a little higher than you could lift your feet with comfort. He was above them now and looking down on the two of them. And his eyes said *Follow me*.

Muddlespot knew he could not even put his foot on the first step. If he did, he would be blasted apart from outside and from within. It just Could Not Be.

And yet . . .

Something within him pulled upwards. It was like a hook, fastened into his breastbone where that arrow had hit. It was a spark that burned inside him and lifted him as it burned. It wasn't fire. (He would have been comfortable with fire.) It was colder than the deepest depths of space. And it tugged at him. It tore. His body was fighting it like a fish on a line, and yet like a fish he was being hauled where he would not and could not go. His feet were on the stair. He could not remember putting them there.

'Good luck,' he heard Sally say. 'We need it.'

He took a step upwards. He felt the stairs shudder beneath his feet as if there were a living thing that recoiled at his touch. He felt the fabric of Creation tremble. And still the spark in his breast tugged him upwards, and he seemed to hear a voice whisper *Yes. Yes, foul though you are, because of this one thing within you, you may rise. You may. If you can.*

Windleberry was above him. He was taking another step.

'Wait!' Muddlespot gasped. 'I'm coming.'

Love is the reason things happen when they shouldn't.

13: CORRIDORS

Where is Heaven?

Up above the clouds? Really?

Up above the clouds (depending on which clouds you mean) there's the stratosphere, where the air is so thin and cold that if you jumped into it you'd freeze and burst at the same time. There's no Heaven there. Try further up.

In the Van Allen belts maybe, ten thousand kilometres above the Earth's surface? This far up there's no atmosphere at all, and enough radiation to fry whatever's left of you after you've done your bursting and freezing.

Not here either, guv.

Come on. It looks like it's further than we thought. Let's get out beyond the orbit of Mars, out beyond those frozen, gassy monsters that we on our little rock presume to call Jupiter, Saturn, Uranus and Neptune. Out to places so far from our sun that it looks like no more than a pinpoint of bright light, to the vast emptiness of the heliosheath that stretches on and on until there's nothing at all. And then . . .

Let's just think about how far it is to the nearest star. The very nearest one. Heaven? Not on this line. Must have got on the wrong train. Go back and take another look at the departure board.

Don't look above the altocumulus and the cirrocumulus. Look above the clouds of Want and Desire. Don't reach for the droplets of water that glisten in the rainbow. Look for the lights of Hope and the colours of Charity. Pass the mists of the Aurora to one side. Rise boldly through the mists of, well, Mystery. There you will find it. The City in the Sky.

It is vast. It stretches farther than the eye can understand. Its walls are higher than thunderclouds, its towers are of pure light, its domes are of moon-glow, its banners are like comet-trails across the sky. A million, million glittering lamps shine from its windows and battlements. Splendour falls on other walls and lights them with the glory of the setting sun.

But this city glows from within, and beside it the Sun itself is the palest candle.

Cue the trumpets, please.

I don't believe it, thought Muddlespot.

He felt like an ant at the gates of the Taj Mahal.

I just don't . . .

I mean I knew it was here, but . . .

It's even bigger than our place. And a *lot* more scary.

'Come on,' muttered Windleberry. 'Don't look as though you are with me. Just keep moving in the same direction as I do.'

The windows in the towers were long, thin and glowing with colour. They looked down upon Muddlespot, blank-eyed, as if they suspected he didn't belong.

There was a crowd at the gate. Above the hub-bub Muddlespot heard the voices of the angels who receive the souls that come up from below. They had eyes of burning coal and swords of fire, and their song was endless. And there was more than a hint of desperation in it.

'Please wait in line,' they chanted endlessly. '*Please* do not crowd the tables. Each of you will receive your results. It's not as though you need to hurry. You're in Eternity now.'

'Where's Saint Peter?' called a voice from the crowd.

'I'm afraid he's busy at the moment,' replied an angel. 'Please do not—'

'Then where's Yama?' cried another.

'He's busy too. Please wait until you are asked to come forward—'

A little beyond the main crush was a line of tables with angels sitting in them. Souls were being waved forward to them one by one.

'Name?' said the angel at the nearest.

'Er – Jeff Coulsever, it was,' said the soul.

'Do you know your results?'

'I beg your pardon?'

'Your examination results,' said the angel patiently, holding out an envelope.

'Results?' said the soul. 'Look, I'm sorry, I'm new here. I didn't know . . .' It opened the envelope nervously. 'Oh.'

'That's not a pass mark, I'm afraid,' said the angel kindly. 'As things stand, we can't admit you. Would you like to appeal?'

The soul was looking through pages and pages

of questions and answers. Its face had turned pale. 'Er . . .' it said.

'You want to take a few moments to think about it?' said the angel.

'Er, yes. Yes, please . . .'

'Sure. Come back when you're ready.'

'Er, thanks.' The soul turned away. Then it turned back again. 'Look, I seem to have answered some of these questions before I was three! I don't even remember—'

'Take your time,' said the angel. 'If you'd like a hint, I'd have a close look at questions two thousand to seven thousand – the module on Love. That's where most appeals get lodged. To tell the truth, there's a bit of a backlog in the Appeals Board at the moment.'

'This is WRONG!' cried another soul, pushing forward. 'This is all wrong! You shouldn't be here!'

'I shouldn't be here?' said the angel.

'None of this should be here! There's no basis for you in science. You're a delusion! I shouldn't have to put up with this. It's insulting!'

'I see,' said the angel. 'And you are . . . ?'

'Dead,' said the soul firmly. 'My heart has stopped beating, my brain has died, all my crucial bodily functions have ceased. I am a mass of tissues, slowly dissipating back into the carbon cycle. And *you* do not exist at all!'

'Are you sure about that?' said the angel woodenly.

'Yes, I'm sure!' snapped the soul, beginning to sound as if it would have liked to be a bit more sure than it really was. 'You're just something happening inside my head as my brain decays. I'm going to shut my eyes and wait for darkness.'

'Would you like to look at your results while you're waiting?'

'No!'

The angel scratched its flaming hair. 'Then I'm afraid I'll have to ask you to stand to one side until my supervisor gets back. He did say he wouldn't be long.'

'It's a disgrace!'

'Look, I'm sorry,' said the angel. 'The fact is, I'm new in this job and all I'm supposed to do is hand out results and tell people if they've passed or not. Could you please—'

'Excuse me,' said the next soul in the queue. 'But could I apply for a resit?'

'Resit?' said the young angel. Things were rapidly getting beyond it.

'Oh yes, you can resit,' said the soul. 'This was

my sixth attempt. I was Amon-Hotep's love slave in ancient Egypt, and when he died my throat was cut so that I could be buried in the pyramid with him. And in my next life I was a Roman centurion in Spain. And then I was an Aztec priest and did human sacrifices in the temple. And then I was a Chinese pirate, and then I was Marie Walewska and was mistress to Napoleon, and then I was a telesales executive in Bristol. I've always been borderline,' the soul finished brightly, 'so I've always been allowed another try.'

'Are you sure about this?' said the angel. Its tone implied that – whatever the love slave and the centurion and the Aztec and the pirate and Ms Walewska had done – the telesales executive's grades were nowhere near borderline and nothing could make them so.

High on a wall was a counter with twelve dials. The dials were made of ebony and the figures on them were inlaid with ash. The first six dials were still, like mourners waiting patiently in a church for a coffin to arrive. They read:

132,658,

Different degrees of movement were discernible on the next four, which read:

The last but one moved steadily as Muddlespot watched,

like that.

The final counter was a blur.

Windleberry had gone. Muddlespot followed, squeezing through the crowd, trying to look as small as possible. He certainly *felt* small. Everything around him was different from anything he had ever known. Where he came from, new arrivals didn't get to answer back. That was for sure.

And yet there was something strangely familiar about what he had just seen. Especially about giving the new man the worst job going. He could almost hear the voice of that angel's older colleague saying,

Mind this table for me, would you? I won't be long, honest.
And if any of them get difficult, just keep asking them if
they're sure. They soon won't be.

He hurried on down a crowded corridor, threading
between bands of penitent souls, clumps of choristers
and some very intimidating-looking wielders of fiery
swords. Where was Windleberry? Up ahead? All these
Fluffies looked the same!

If they saw who he was . . .

Just keep going, he told himself. In some ways this
place *is* like being Down Below. When you get sent
someplace where they don't know you and you want
to come out alive. The rules are: (1) don't go there;
(2) if you really have to go there, then *look busy*. Look
as if you know what you are doing. Look, above all, as
if messing with you will bring trouble from someone
very big and very powerful.

It worked – some of the time anyway. Maybe it
would work here too.

'Sorry,' he said, bumping against someone. He
hurried on before whoever it was looked down and
wondered why they had a smear of flesh-coloured
paint on their arm. 'Sorry.'

As he went he repeated over to himself the
directions Windleberry had given him in case of

separation. The thirteenth hall. The Stair of a Thousand Steps. The Chamber of Stars. The Gallery of Green Sunsets . . .

Had he got it in the right order?

What if he got lost here?

Exactly how long was he going to get away with this, sweating up and down these corridors, dripping paint and with his tail all knotted up and literally between his legs? And dodging round Fluffies at every turn?

But Windleberry had been right about one thing.

They were all averting their eyes.

'All right,' said Miss Ogle, Form Tutor to 9c. 'Who has seen Imogen's oboe?'

9c sat before her in four rows and silence.

'This is *important*,' said Miss Ogle. 'She has an exam this afternoon. We don't want her to miss it, do we?'

Silence.

Silence, but the sort of silence you could read if you knew how. Sally, sitting at the back (and still smarting from getting her first 'Late' *ever*) could read it like a book.

Eva and Holly were sitting bolt upright at the table

before her. It wasn't us, the set of their shoulders said. Though we might have done it if we'd thought of it.

Cassie and Viola were one table to the left of them. Sally couldn't see their faces either, but she could just catch the look that Viola threw sideways at Holly. *It ***** well was you*, that look said. *And when we're through with you you'll be wishing you'd gone to hospital in the ambulance yesterday too.*

The boys were glancing at each other. Girl stuff, their eyes said. Stay out. Less fun than putting your hand in a hornets' nest, definitely.

Imogen's head was bowed, weighed down with the thought that everyone in the class hated her. This couldn't be happening. She was Public Enemy Number One. She was going to miss her exam. Her parents were going to—

And Janey, at the table by the door, was looking Miss Ogle innocently in the eye.

Yep, Sally could read it like a book.

Miss Ogle couldn't.

'I'm waiting,' she said.

Silence.

Half the class was thinking: Why couldn't she have played the clarinet? Plenty of clarinets at school she could have borrowed.

Just about everybody else was thinking: Keep quiet. Stay out. She'll soon realize . . .

A hand went up.

'Yes, Minnie?'

Oh, no.

'Um. Miss Ogle?' said Minnie (still with her hand in the air) . . .

No, Minnie. *No!*

'. . . I think it's something to do with Billie and Viola.'

Beyond the Chamber of Stars, down the Gallery of Green Sunsets, through the little door behind the one hundred and fifty-fourth pillar in the Hall of Butterfly Wings, there a was a narrow corridor with no name at all. Halfway down it there was a door with a sign:

Cupids *can* spell. They just don't want it known. Inside the Store room was another sign.

The store clerk was a cupid. He looked at the requisition that Muddlespot handed to him.

'Nope,' he said.

'It's in order, isn't it?' said Muddlespot, sidling closer so that as much of him as possible was concealed behind the counter. Cupids, he had noticed, did *not* avert their eyes, and now that he was in close proximity to one his disguise was feeling very thin indeed.

'Nope,' said the cupid again.

'I'm sure it *is*,' said Muddlespot, who had spent a good hour down in Sally's mind watching while Windleberry very carefully wrote out, copied, signed, sealed and resealed the parchment specifying exactly what it was that had to be collected from the cupids' stores.

'Can't let you have anything on this,' said the cupid firmly. 'Not been countersigned, see?'

'The countersignature is over the page,' said Muddlespot sweetly.

'Don't make any difference,' said the cupid

194

promptly. *'Still can't let you have that thing.'*

Again that feeling! Never mind the constant harp music, the lack of bloodstains on the walls and the air smelling of sunsets rather than seared flesh. If you got sent to the stores Down Below – say for a number five burner or something – this was exactly the conversation you would have there.

'Stores is for storing,' said the cupid. *'You want something issued, you has to go to "Issues", see?'*

There is a certain sort of practical joke that minor officials everywhere play on people they think were born yesterday. They actually find it funny. It brightens their miserable lives.

'Right . . .'

And by the standards of eternity, Muddlespot had indeed been born yesterday. If not in the last five minutes.

'. . . I see . . .'

But he had *also* been born in a place where you either learned *very* quickly or you quickly stopped learning altogether.

'And that's where they keep the left-handed hammers and the stripy paint, is it?' he said, looking the cupid hard in the eye.

'Could be.' The cupid shrugged and shifted his

gaze. He sniffed the air. A frown crossed his face.

Muddlespot sidled closer still. Perhaps he shouldn't have said the word 'paint'. Where was Windleberry?

The door behind him banged open. Another cupid rushed in, carrying a huge sheaf of papers. His cheeks were pink from fluttering at speed. He slammed a requisition down on the counter.

'Here,' he said. 'Need it quick.'

The store-cupid looked at the new demand and frowned again. He shook his head slowly. 'Can't . . .'

'It's for the Appeal. Erry says.' He pointed to the signature at the bottom of the page.

Whoever had signed it hadn't much liked paperwork, thought Muddlespot. They had crossed their signature out, put it in the wrong box and drawn three smiley faces and a load of hearts in the margin. Even so, it seemed to have more effect than Windleberry's carefully correct script. Scowling, the store-cupid turned and disappeared deep among the shelves. There followed the unmistakable sounds of locks being unlocked, traps being tripped and three-headed fire-breathing dogs being muzzled, before the cupid returned (lightly singed and bitten) to the counter.

'There you go,' he said sulkily.

He placed it on the board. A cupid arrow, tipped

with a heart-shaped head. Something in Muddlespot's breastbone ached at the sight of it. But unlike the ones he had seen flashing through the chambers of Sally's mind, this one did not glitter. It was dull and grey. It was not even particularly sharp-looking.

'Hey . . . !' said Muddlespot.

'Cheers!' said the pink cupid and flew out of the door.

Muddlespot stared at the store-cupid. 'But that was exactly what I was—'

'Yes?' said the cupid expressionlessly.

'But *I* wanted—'

Muddlespot checked himself. He looked at the cupid. The cupid looked back. Muddlespot took a deep breath.

'Uh, never mind,' he said. 'Issues, you say? I'll go and ask. Sorry to have bothered you . . .'

He left. He closed the door. Down the corridor the pink cupid was still in sight, fluttering erratically onwards with the leaden arrow in his hands. Muddlespot hurried after him. On tiptoe.

There *was* one way, he thought, in which Up Here was not like Down Below.

Here, they did turn their backs on you.

*

At the end of registration Miss Ogle took Billie and Viola and Minnie and Imogen down to see Mr Singh. Soberly, the rest of the class gathered their things and prepared to get on with the day. They knew that this wasn't the end of it. For a start, Minnie would have to be caught in the corridors at some point and executed by firing squad. But now even the teachers would know that something was up. They'd try to do something about it.

In the corridor, Sally put on a spurt and caught up with Janey.

'Hey?' she said.

'Hm?'

'That oboe . . .'

Janey's face was blank. 'Nothing to do with me.'

'Sure. But do you think she'll get it back before her exam?'

Still blank. 'Probably not.'

Still blank, but with just that edge to her voice that said – don't push me, Sally. Janey was a good person. She could also break arms.

'It kind of raises the stakes, though, doesn't it?'

'How do you mean?'

'Missing an exam. There won't be another chance for months. Her parents will have paid money . . .'

And Imogen probably wouldn't make Grade 8 before GCSEs hit. That sort of thing mattered, in that sort of family.

Janey frowned. 'Tough for her.'

'It's just that . . .'

'WHAT?'

Janey didn't like doing bad to people. She hated getting caught doing it. Sally looked her in the eye.

'It's going to have to go back sometime, isn't it . . . ?'

If it didn't go back it would be theft. But Sally didn't say that. She didn't have to. Janey bent her head and walked on, frowning.

'I'm sure it'll turn up,' she said.

'Yeah. How?'

'Somehow.'

'I mean – it can't just be given back, can it? Because they'll think whoever gives it back must have been the person who took it in the first place.'

Janey stalked on. She said nothing. Sally followed. They came to the lockers. Janey opened hers, put in her books and took out the books for the next lesson. There was no oboe in the locker. Tight-lipped, Sally got her books out too. Other pupils were clustering around their locker doors, chattering, unearthing books, exclaiming at how *stupid* Minnie had been. Sally stepped up close to Janey.

'Bit of a problem?' she said.

Janey's jaw tightened. She was fed up with Sally. She was fed up with Imogen. Maybe she was a bit fed up with Ameena too, now. She didn't like the role she was playing.

'Got any ideas?' she said.

'Might have.'

Janey turned to the next locker. It was Ameena's. The padlock had a combination. Janey knew it. She undid it and left the lock hanging open.

'Yours,' she said, and walked off with her bag over her shoulder.

Sally hung back as the other kids flooded off to their classrooms. As the last one turned the corner she slipped the open padlock from its bracket and looked into Ameena's locker.

There it was.

14: GUILTY

Another thing about Up Here was that you didn't see many people dragging inert victims around the place. So far Muddlespot had only spotted one. That had been himself, hauling the stunned cupid by the heels past a Mirror of Harmony just now. It made him feel even more conspicuous.

He was beginning to sweat. He knew that because the floor had started feeling sticky every time he put a foot down. He was panicky and confused. Every professional instinct was screaming at him to reach down and rend his victim limb from limb (this was the accepted procedure back home). But he wasn't at home. This was not Pandemonium. Up here, in this endless palace of light and music and order, even the smallest pile of entrails was going to start people asking questions.

He would have gone through the cupid's pockets, only being a cupid it didn't have any.

He dragged the body over to the wall and concealed it behind a thick tapestry of Calm. Then he hurried back to the point where he had made his attack and scooped up the arrow that the cupid had let fall. Well, that was Step One of the mission completed. Fifty per cent success rate so far, which was infinity per cent more than he had been expecting. Step Two was to get away with it.

He gathered up the cupid's papers in case they attracted attention. He glanced at the top one.

Yer Brief

1. Deny Everything. Keep doing this.

'You bet,' he muttered.

2. Blame Other Departments.

3. Deny Everything again.

4. Wait for yer chance. Soon as the B♥ggers get inter one of their barneys 'bout guilt an' sin an' redemshun an' stuff, yer goes an' leans on ther evvydense table. Yer swaps ther lead arrow fer the gold'un, quick like. THEN when they next looks at yer, yer can say oh but it wozzn't a gold arrow we shot, it woz ther lead 'un which don't make ther victim fall in luv it does ther other fing. So it wuz ALL misunnerstanding. Gettit?

P.S. DON'T GET CAUGHT or yer cushions. Erry says.

'Change of plan,' said Muddlespot. 'Swapping arrows – bad idea. You just stick with points one to three and you'll be all right. When you wake up.'

He hurried off to look for Windleberry.

Windleberry was not in the Hall of Ten Thousand Columns, where a choir was beginning to tune up for a practice. He was not in the Gallery of Green Sunsets, where angels flowed busily to and fro on a myriad of different errands. He was not in the Chamber of Stars, which was absolutely crowded with—

'Oi!' called a voice. Muddlespot looked around. Mistake.

A cupid was fluttering down the corridor towards him. Muddlespot clutched the huge sheaf of papers to himself, sheltering behind them as far as he could.

This cupid too was out of breath.

'You seen Spikey?' Its eye fell on the arrow and papers. 'He give you those?'

Muddlespot's brain, fired by terror, moved at lightning speed. 'Spikey' must be the pink cupid who was now slumbering peacefully behind the tapestry in the corridor outside the Dept of Luv Stors.

'He – er – took a break,' said Muddlespot.

'Took a break? Cheeky bugger! Got you to stand in for him, did he? I bet. Who are you, anyway? I've not seen you before.'

'I'm, er, I'm new.'

The cupid blew out his fat cheeks. 'This ain't one fer a newbie. Spikey should know that. I'll twist his neck when I catch him.'

His neck's a bit fat, actually, thought Muddlespot. I went for the back of the head myself.

'I'll handle it,' he said as brightly as he could.

'I'm *ever* so eager to please. Just point me in the right direction and leave me to it.'

'Point you? Boy, I'm *taking* you. You don't arrive and do like you should it'll be my neck that gets twisted. Come on – we're late!'

'Oh no, really, I'm quite sure I can handle it . . .'

'Come on! cried the cupid, fluttering a little ahead of him. 'They won't wait – Hey! What happened to yer wings?'

'Wings?'

Some aspects of Muddlespot's disguise were really rather weak. Some didn't exist at all.

'I've – er – I've been grounded,' he said desperately, waddling after the cupid as fast as he could.

The cupid cackled. 'Yer can't be *that* new, then.'

'Are you sure of that . . . ?'

As he ran, Muddlespot's eyes flicked left and right, searching for a way of escape. If he could just lose himself in the crowd, somehow? But that was going to be tricky, when the cupid could fly and he couldn't. Maybe he should wait for some lonely corridor somewhere.

Trouble was, there didn't seem to be any. Every room or hall or chamber they entered seemed to be larger than the last, and with more and more people in it. They seemed to be heading towards the centre of things.

'Er – where are we going?'

'Din't he tell yer ANYFING? Appeals Board, of course.'

The boys had been sent off to P.E. The girls had been kept back. Mr Singh had been called in. Things were getting predictable.

'. . . Now it *seems* that there have been some things that are *very silly* going on,' Mr Singh was saying as he paced up and down the rows. 'I am very *disappointed* to hear about it. It seems that *some people* are not living up to the standards that we expect at this school . . .'

One to one Mr Singh was quite effective. He was all turban and bushy brows and seamlessly interwoven moustache and beard and 100% eye contact. He talked, you listened.

Put him in front of fifteen girls at once, though, and he wouldn't manage to make eye contact with any of them. He would march up and down to the sound of his own voice while fifteen girls waited until he finished. Then he would nod and walk out again.

'. . . Respect for one another. And also for their

property. To remove the property of another pupil without their permission is *theft*. Even if the intention is to return it at some point . . .'

Sally knew she should just sit it out. She always had done before.

'. . . *very* seriously. I assure you I am not joking . . .'

Except for one thing. Before, she had always been innocent.

'. . . I very much hope, indeed I *expect*, that that musical instrument will be returned before four o'clock. It is a *very serious thing* to cause a fellow pupil to miss an exam . . .'

As long as he was still marching up and down and talking, Sally thought, it was OK. And when it got to 'I-expect-anyone-who-knows-anything-about-this-to-come-and-see-me' it was probably still OK. But if they got on to searching the corridors before the next break it was going to be bad. Stashing the oboe in her locker hadn't been a clever thing to do. She had been totally focused on getting it off Janey, and by the time she had done that there hadn't been a moment to think what to do next.

Theft. He had said it.

If she just handed it over to Imogen, or indeed to Mr Singh, everyone would think it was Billie or Holly or someone like that who had taken it, even if they didn't think it was Sally herself. There would be some tough questions. And not answering tough questions when asked would mean Big Trouble. She *had* to find a way of covering her tracks. She couldn't think of one.

I'm no good at this, she thought. I'm only good at being good.

Her palms were prickling and her throat felt tight. If he stopped and looked at her. And she looked back . . .

Janey could look innocent when she wasn't. Everyone else could.

Sally didn't know how to.

'. . . I need hardly say that there will be the **most serious consequences . . .'**

It was unreal. It was like being in a dream, just as it starts to turn into a nightmare. The room around her seemed to be huge. The ceiling was almost out of sight, lifted high above her on great marble columns. White marble benches circled around her, rising like flights of giant steps, and all of them were empty except for the very highest row where a huge, brooding presence looked down upon her with eyes of ice. She felt very small.

And for some reason, she also felt very sticky.

Words seemed to float before her, written on a page she held. They said: Deny everything.

Somewhere a voice was speaking, as if from a dream. She could not quite hear the words that it was saying. But she knew what they must be.

It's all your fault, isn't it? You started all of this.

Deny everything. She couldn't possibly do that. She didn't know how.

It *is* all your fault, isn't it? the voice insisted. **It *was* you.**

Yes, she whispered in her mind. Yes, it is. Guilty.

'Guilty!' squeaked Muddlespot.

There was a huge, shocked silence.

'What're yer *doin*?' hissed the cupid beside him.

Muddlespot could not answer. He could not think. He could only look up, and around, at all that huge chamber and the presences within it, centred upon him where he stood quivering in the witness stand.

(Well, not exactly *on* him. Even now the attention, though keenly focused, remained averted from the point of greatest interest.)

There were the vast, living statues, soaring all the

way up to the row of six eyes that peered down like eagles from a cliff-side nest.

There was the woman standing on the platform, with an angel at her side. Both seemed suddenly to have woken up and started to pay him attention.

There was the *huge* angel in the galleries, dark-robed, dark-winged and with eyes that sent bluots of chill through Muddlespot's spine. Muddlespot had felt his presence looming there the moment he had scuttled into the courtroom. He felt it now, bearing down upon him, suddenly intent, like a hunter who has seen something twitch among the grasses. Muddlespot was trying to look everywhere but up. Even so he knew that angel was there.

'**The Witness is not required to enter a plea . . .**' came a voice from high among the heads of the columns.

'But on a point of order, your Graces,' said the great angel.

He said it in a voice of such cold calm that it got even the living statues' attention.

'The Statement of the Witness would seem to require clarification. Are we to understand that his Department now accepts responsibility for the answers given to, I believe, 2304(a) through to 6823(d) iii, including the questions on Adultery, Illegal Marriage, War and Destruction . . . ?'

All eyes were on (or near) Muddlespot. His mouth was open, his limbs were locked in terror. He had barely heard what was being said.

To make it worse, in his efforts to avoid looking up at the dark angel, he had glanced to his right and found that there was one set of eyes in the courtroom that were definitely *not* averted. They belonged to a grey-skinned fiend from Pandemonium, seated on the lower benches, who was leaning forward and staring at him. Its gaze seemed to peel back his layers of flesh-coloured paint, as if it suspected something that no one else did.

Somewhere far away a voice seemed to be checking over the list. War, yes. Destruction, yes. Illegal Marriage, pretty much. Adultery – well, no, but that's a detail . . .

The voice sounded like Sally.

'Yes!' Muddlespot squeaked. 'Yes we do. It was our fault. We admit it. Everything!'

'Wot the . . . ! ? !' hissed the cupid beside him.

Deny everything, whispered the papers that he clutched to his chest.

Too late.

'But . . .' said the smaller angel who stood beside

the woman on the platform. 'But – if we understand the witness correctly – then I submit, Your Graces, that my client has after all no case to answer?' He sounded as though he could hardly believe it himself.

There was a long and heavy silence.

'It would seem not,' said the Voice From On High.

The cupid swore, once, and flew out through the exit like a bumblebee on turbo.

'*And* that my clients have a claim for redress for wrongful detention, false witness, defamation of character, personal distress, official misconduct and misdirection in each and every one of forty-one hearings over three thousand years?' said the angel on the platform, gathering speed as it emerged from its state of surprise.

'Don't push your luck,' said the Voice From On High.

The silence returned.

'This testimony bears on many cases,' said the Voice From On High. **'There are Implications to Consider. The Court will Adjourn.'**

Uproar! Voices from everywhere! Angels that were Counsels, Clerks and Ushers, Callers and Trumpeters and Scriveners and Scruplers all appeared in a shining throng and began arguing furiously with each other about what it all meant. The doors burst open and in rushed a whole host of other Guardians who had spent the last three thousand years waiting for their own humans' cases to be heard, and they all cheered the Guardian on the witness stand and slapped it on the back and tossed it in the air to cries of 'Hip, Hip Hoorah!' and 'For he's a Jolly Good Angel . . .' and so on. The sudden turmoil tumbled Muddlespot from his place. He was knocked this way, pushed that, lost his footing and found himself crammed up against a table made of rose petals, on which rested an arrow exactly like the one he held in his hand except that its head was gold. The part of his brain that had not completely lost the plot (about 10% of it) remembered that it was here for some reason to do with collecting arrows. Signals fired urgently to his jaw (which was the only part of him capable of gathering anything because his arms, feet and tail were all variously committed at the time). He snatched it in his teeth and squirmed away through the crowd.

Behind him, the woman on the platform looked around. There was a question in her eyes, but no one spoke to her.

Slowly she took a step from her place. Then

another. Then she walked down the stairs and quietly out through the doors: out into Heaven at last, after three thousand years. Behind her on the platform the marks of her feet remained, worn into the stone over the centuries of shifting her weight from one to the other while she waited for her judgement to pass.

In the gallery a slow smile spread over the face of the dark angel.

15: THE ARROW OF LEAD

Bells were ringing. Announcements being sung in urgent harmonies by unseen voices in mid-air. Councils were being called. A pulse of excitement swelled outwards from the Appeals Chamber and ran down the million passages of Heaven, shaking the saints from their contemplations and knocking the doves from their perches. Loud shrieks were heard emanating from the Tower of Love.

Far down the corridors of the Department of Geography, Mishamh heard the commotion. He could not think what it meant. He had never heard anything like it in Heaven before. For a moment he was lost for words. This was bad news because he was taking a class at the time.

Before him, sitting in their neat ranks and rows of a

hundred by a hundred, the souls sensed his hesitation. Immediately a soft murmur rose among them. Eyes went to windows. One actually went to the great double doors of the classroom and peered out. Others craned to see.

Mishamh rapped his desk sternly with the board rubber, rousing a small nebula of stardust.

'I repeat: the distance from the Sun in which life can exist ranges from eighty-eight million miles to one hundred and thirty million miles from the Sun's surface, that is, less than zero-point-zero-two per cent of the distance to the outermost edge of the solar system. Write it down . . .

'And the atmospheric pressure that humans could possibly stand ranges from a few kilometres above to a few kilometres below Earth's sea level. That is less than zero-point-two per cent of the distance from the centre of the earth to the outermost edge of the Earth's atmosphere.'

He liked to pause at this point, to give souls who had managed to live their entire lives without once considering how small and precarious was the bubble in which the whole of human history was taking place a chance to see what was coming.

'Therefore, the slightest alteration in conditions

surrounding the planet would lead to the extinction of all . . .'

The doors slammed open. An angel from the Department of Geography stood in the doorway. A ripple ran through the benches. (This class of souls were still in their first century in Heaven and had yet to settle down properly to the serious business of study.)

'Doomsday's sent for you,' said the angel to Mishamh.

'But my lesson . . .'

'I'm to take it,' said the angel. 'He wants you down at the Appeals Board. Something's happening.'

Behind him, the unusual murmurs swelled in the corridors of Heaven. More souls had tiptoed to the door now, peering out to see what was happening.

'Cupids!' cried one in sudden alarm. 'Everyone hide!'

At once ten thousand souls dived under the benches and tables. Most of them had been nicked by a cupid at some point in their careers. None of them now felt the experience worth repeating.

'Hurry!' said the angel.

The Lobby of the Law was alive with angels, flapping

and hurrying and buzzing about how everything in Heaven had suddenly been turned upon its head. Muddlespot dodged among them, hiding in the press of people, ducking between legs and under wings. He was knocked this way and then that, tossed like a cork in a high sea. He saw an exit – a hall of pillars that receded into the distance. He struggled towards it. He was sent spinning by a rush of gabbling trumpeters, lost sight of it, saw it again – or maybe it was another that looked just like it. He squeezed between a Choirmaster and a Scribe and scuttled forward. He was nearly there . . .

Ouch! Fierce taloned hands seized him from behind. He was spun round and slammed bodily into a pillar. Dazed, he looked up.

Two red eyes, set in a grey, leathery face and smouldering like globs of molten lava, looked down upon him.

'Just a minute,' hissed the fiend from Pandemonium. 'I'd like a little word with you.'

'I . . .' gasped Muddlespot.

'Y'see,' it whispered. '*I've* got this strange idea you might not be what you seem to be. What's this? Paint? Thought so. So what's *underneath*, then?'

'I . . . er . . . secret mission?' Muddlespot ventured.

'So? But you won't mind telling *me*, about it, will you? Three thousand years I've been waiting here – for nothing! You won't mind coming back down the hole a little bit? Then we can get the squeezers out and have a *nice* long talk about it. And you know what? I really hope it's a very, very special mission. Because I'm going to be soooo disappointed if it isn't . . .'

'I can't!' squeaked Muddlespot. 'I've got to—'

'Oh, yes you can. In fact, I think you really *want* to.'

He didn't want to. He very much didn't want to. If there was one thing even more dangerous than being with the Fluffies it was being with someone from his own side after he had upset them. The fiend was way bigger than him. It had him by both arms and was marching him along. His feet scrabbled on the floor of the Lobby, but the Lobby was of marble and polished to a high degree. He slid. The fiend was working him around the edge of the crowd, back towards the court. He could see the great space opening up beyond the doors. He could see the huge hole in the floor. He was going to have to think of something quickly.

In fact, make that Very Quickly.

Like, *now*.

Think, Muddlespot! Think, if you want to stay joined to your arms and legs!! Think, think, think . . .

Oh-help-oh-help-oh-help-oh . . .

'Sorry!' cried a young angel, receding rapidly down the pillared hall. In his wake he left Muddlespot spinning like a top. The fiend, who had taken the full force of the impact, lay flat and still on the marble floor.

Bruised but happy, breathing hard, Mishamh caught up with Doomsday. He was ready for a rebuke but none came. His chief paced down the corridors of Heaven with the slow majesty of a thundercloud. Lesser angels exploded from his path like frightened doves and gathered to whisper excitedly in the balconies.

'This asteroid of yours . . .' said Doomsday.

'Still on course, sir.'

'Is it? I thought we had decided to divert.'

'I was waiting until the cancellation order actually came through.'

'I see. Quite right, as it happens. The Appeal has been decided, on terms that will allow the backlog to be cleared quickly. Once we get back to the office, you had better summon the staff.'

'Decided? Then . . . do you think Zebukun will actually happen, sir?'

'It seems so. If that's what the Governors want.'

'But we know they do, don't we? They set the deadline. They set the Great Curriculum and the Heavenly Laws. They have to follow their own Laws, sir.'

'You would think, wouldn't you?'

'Up, quick,' said a voice.

Muddlespot, dazed and nearly senseless, remembered it from somewhere. 'Mmmmuuurghghghgh,' he said. He was surprised by his own eloquence.

Square fingers caught him by the nape of the neck. Powerful muscles heaved. The marble floor gathered itself under the soles of his feet. The face of Windleberry appeared before him. Around them the great pillared hallway had emptied, apart from the grey-skinned fiend lying stunned and still.

'Where – where have you been?' groaned Muddlespot.

'Never far. You have the arrow?'

'Uh – two of them, I think.' Still dazed, Muddlespot held out the things he had been clutching to his chest.

Silently Windleberry took the sheaf of papers and dropped them on the floor. Then he took Muddlespot's other hand, prised the fingers open and eased the two arrows from the little fiend's locked, shocked grasp.

'Now – can you move? This one will be coming round in a moment.'

Indeed the fiend was beginning to twitch where it lay and to make 'mmuuurghghgh' sort of noises itself. Muddlespot put one foot in front of the other. He swayed.

'I think . . .' He swayed some more.

'Come on,' said Windleberry.

Muddlespot put his hand against the marble wall. 'You go on,' he groaned. 'I'm done for.'

'Only if you insist.'

'That's not very nice!' snarled Muddlespot, lifting his head. 'Aren't you supposed to say something like "I'm not leaving without you?"'

'If you like.'

'I do like.'

'And then I stun you with one chop of my hand and carry you out of the city on my back?'

'No!'

'I could do it.'

He would too, thought Muddlespot. He's so good, he's absolutely bloody ruthless. And that's . . .

. . . that's why I love him.

'I'll try,' he said.

'Hurry!'

Muddlespot tried to hurry. Flesh-coloured footprints wove in erratic patterns on the marble floor behind him.

'Faster!' said Windleberry, flying above.

'I can't!'

'You must run!'

'I can't . . .'

'THERE HE IS!!!!'

A cloud of cupids, buzzing like angry wasps, wove into the lobby behind them. Some of them had weapons. Among them was a very pink looking cupid with a bandage around his head. And also the cupid who had led Muddlespot to the court. He was pointing an accusing finger now, down the columnar perspectives of the Great Hall, straight at Muddlespot's heart.

'*Run!*' screamed Muddlespot, and found that he could.

'Left at the end!' cried Windleberry. 'Make for the wall!'

'Oi-oi-oi-oi-oi!!!!' called the cupids from behind them. 'Get them! Trespassers!!! Close the Gates!!!'

'Tresp . . .' (gasp) '. . . passers?' Muddlespot's legs were going like the running wheel of a hamster on steroids. His breath couldn't keep up.

'Technical . . .' (gasp) 'term,' said Windleberry, also going as fast as he could. 'Use it . . . a lot . . . up here.'

'Where . . . were you . . . anyway? Lost . . . you.'

'Had to . . . keep out of . . . sight of . . . cupids. Didn't want to be . . . recognized.'

They wheeled out of the corridor into a wide cloister peopled with silent, contemplative robed figures and scattered them in all directions.

'How are you . . . doing on . . . that, then?'

'Oi-oi-oi-oi-oi!!!! It's Windleberry!!! Unleash the doves!!!!'

'May have . . . blown it . . . Left here!'

They crashed through a crowd of praying figures, showering the air with scriptures and prayer mats, caught a couple of mats as they fell and ski-ed across a Pool of Contemplation before the mats could realize what they were doing and sink. A line of battlements blocked their way. Towers loomed over them. From the tops figures looked down, pointing. Bells were ringing. The air flustered with fierce and restless feathers. Behind them, the whole swarm of cupids came hallooing into view. Before them . . .

'*Jump!*' cried Windleberry.

. . . was nothing but blue air, golden clouds moving, the wall of the city falling to impossible depths beneath them, the sudden, stomach-sickening feeling of being somewhere very very very high up and the signals firing urgently through Muddlespot's brain screaming: *Don't Jump! Whatever you do, don't . . .*

He already had.

A
A
A
A
A
A
A
A
A
A
A
.
.
;

(Time now for a quick commercial break. Buy
Heavenly Snackers. They're *the* Organic, Fairtrade,

Vegan-friendly, Sugar-Free, responsibly farmed breakfast meal, and each one in the shape of a halo for
your little dear ones to try on. Heavenly Snackers.
Guaranteed to last on your shelf for a lifetime.)

A
A
A
A
A
A
A
A
A
A
A
A
A

A
R
G
H
H
!!
!!'

Thump! as Windleberry's arms closed around Muddlespot. An explosion of air brakes as his wings battled the terrible pull of gravity. The ground was still rushing closer, closer. Maybe their descent was slowing. Maybe they wouldn't be vaporized by the impact after all. Maybe they would just be turned into something that looked like thinly-spread strawberry jam. Maybe they'd . . .

Touch

down.

'There,' said Windleberry. 'That wasn't so bad, was it?'

'My hero,' said Muddlespot weakly. 'Where are we?'

'Period four, it seems. English Literature.'

Muddlespot looked around.

They were standing on a huge, level plateau, broken here and there by large, square-sided outcrops in different colours and surrounded by mountains. Somewhere very far away someone was chanting.

> 'But with unhurrying chase,
> And unperturbèd pace,
> Deliberate speed, majestic instancy . . .'

He recognized that voice. That was how Mr Kingsley thought poetry should be read. And how he tried to make everybody in the class read it.

> 'They beat – and a Voice beat
> More instant than the feet –
> "All things betray thee, who betrayest Me."'

(One of the many bits of advice that Low Command gives its agents on Earth is that the soul is most vulnerable to the little evil whisper when it is under conditions of stress. Therefore, take advantage of this.)

'I pleaded, outlaw-wise,
By many a hearted casement, curtained red,
Trellised with intertwining charities . . .'

(Muddlespot had often thought he should be able to take more advantage of Mr Kingsley's reading.)

He looked around and knew where he was. The plateau he was standing on was the surface of a table in room C23 in Darlington High School. The square outcrops were the books of the pupils, scattered here and there and in some cases even open. The mountains were the pupils themselves, huge figures compared to Muddlespot and Windleberry. He recognized Billie, doodling angrily on a pad of paper on the other side of the room. He saw Sally, rising high above him, looking as though she was paying attention to every word of the reading. Probably she really was. The sight of her face looming up there made him almost misty-eyed with thoughts of comfort and safety.

'You go ahead,' said Windleberry. 'I'm going to meet someone.'

'Who?'

Windleberry pointed towards the mountain that was Billie. 'My colleague. Her Guardian.'

'Ah.' Muddlespot wondered for a moment if he shouldn't warn Scattletail that the twins' Guardians were getting together. But loyalty among fiends is never very strong. At best, it's more an alliance of convenience. And besides, none of this was really about the war between Above and Below. It was more an internal thing on the Above side.

What Muddlespot really wanted right now was to go somewhere where people weren't chasing him, and to get every last spot of flesh-coloured paint off his skin.

'You wanted the arrows for her?' he asked.

'Partly.'

'What are you going to do with them?'

'Improve things.'

'I see,' said Muddlespot. 'Are you going to explain how?'

'When I get back. And another thing. If I find you've been talking to Sally while I'm out . . .'

'Would I?'

'Yes, you would.'

'Oh, all right. Maybe I would. But just this once, I'll have other things to do.'

'Like what?'

'I never thought I'd say this. But I'm going to get washed.'

High upon the battlements of Heaven the Angel of Love walked. She looked down upon the Earth, upon Darlington High, upon two tiny figures making their way in different directions across a tabletop in room C23. Behind her the Celestial clamour had settled down into a more orderly hum. It was an excited, expectant noise. Souls were trickling into the Appeals Chamber with the steady speed of sand through an hourglass. Swiftly their cases were heard, found to be consistent with the New Precedent, and soon the souls were emerging bright-eyed on the far side with their new satchels and their floor plans and their directions to find their lockers and the classrooms of the Department of Love. Thick, purple clouds were gathering over the Towers of Geography, where the Angel of Doomsday was meeting with his team. The numbers of Heavenly exam markers had been doubled to be ready for when the big rush came. Even now the Heavenly Architects were swaying a batch of Celestial portakabins into place outside the Gates of Pearl to act as temporary classrooms until such time as someone could organize the construction of more permanent facilities. And every one was marked 'Department of Love'.

She looked her troops up and down. Every off-duty cupid was present and armed to the teeth. Some had their bows and their arrows. Some had brought their harps and fiddles. Others had bombs of carefully primed rose petals. Still others had machine guns, hand grenades, rocket launchers and garrotting wires, all of which were loaded or tipped or edged or generally reinforced at the business end with gold. Someone had even brought out the old wrecking ball. They looked at her, grim-faced.

Angels do get upset. They do get angry. They call it 'Wrath' but it means the same thing. They don't get much chance to practise it in the normal course of things. But they know how to do it when the time comes.

Let us go, Erry, the eyes of the cupids pleaded. *Give the word. We'll waste 'em. There won't be nuffin' left. You can count on that.*

Erry looked them up and down. Wrath was in her heart too. Cold, bitter, implacable wrath. It made her jaw ache and her toenails curl.

'We will do this my way,' she said softly.

'The ways of Heaven,' said Windleberry, 'are beyond human understanding.'

He had returned to the central chamber of Sally's mind. Sally was there, sitting at her desk, but mentally what she was sitting on was not a chair but a large oboe case, which twitched and glowed and occasionally sent out muffled shrieks such as ♪*'Thief!'*, ♫*'Guilty'* and ♪*'Here I am –* ♫*Come and find me!'*

Muddlespot was there too, wallowing in a large bath of warm water that Sally had obligingly imagined for him. He was scrubbing away at the remaining bits of paint on those areas of himself that it was possible to reach. 'If they're anything like our ways,' he said happily, 'they're beyond *all* understanding. Even we sometimes don't—'

'They are nothing like your ways,' said Windleberry frostily.

♪*'Thief!'*♫ cried the oboe case.

'Shut up,' said Sally.

'So you've given the leaden arrow to your man Ismael,' said Muddlespot, 'And he's going to use it on Billie next time she sees Tony?'

'It won't be that simple,' said Sally. 'Not if I know Billie.'

'Here I ♪am!' chirped the oboe case.

'Shut up,' said Sally. 'Someone will hear you.'

'No,' said Windleberry. 'The leaden arrow is only permitted in the most extreme cases. Neither Ismael nor I would use it on Billie. I gave Ismael the golden arrow, for him to use as he sees fit. As you said, another arrow, another boy. That was not why we went to Heaven.'

Muddlespot sat up with a splash. 'Well that's nice! What did we go all that way for, then?'

'Guil♪ty!♪'

'SHUT UP!' cried Sally, Windleberry and Muddlespot all at once.

♪'meep,'♪ said the oboe case. Its lower catch trembled tearfully.

Muddlespot's eyes narrowed. 'So what happened to the arrow of lead?'

'I have it here,' said Windleberry, producing it. 'And also this.' He produced a short bow with curvy ends. He strung it and plucked the string. It hummed. The gentle note lingered in the air.

'Where did that come from?'

'The cupids dropped it when they last came visiting.

235

You will remember that they left in a hurry. They dropped several, in fact.' Deftly he placed the leaden arrow on the string and drew it back. 'Stay still.'

'What are you . . . ?' Muddlespot's eyes widened in horror. 'No, Windleberry! Not me! You can't—'

'It won't hurt – much.'

'You don't understand!' cried Muddlespot, frantically trying to hide behind a heap of soapsuds. 'I love you, Windleberry. Nothing can stop me loving you—'

'Yes it can!'

'. . . Please! I'm nothing but love for you. If I don't love you I am nothing – don't you see? You're my light, my living, my meaning – there's nothing for me without you. My angel, truly my angel, you can't—'

Twangg – THUMP!

'. . . You BASTARD!!!'

'You see?' said Windleberry. 'I told you it would work.'

16: THE MASK OF EROS

An oboe case.

What is it?

Just a small, black container of hard plastic, with a handle and cheap metal fastenings, and inside something that was once part of a tree. How could it possibly matter so much?

Skill made the oboe. Music could come from it, stirring the soul to soar or to weep. But there were many instruments scattered in their cases around the Music block, and most were a lot bigger than this one.

It *was* the only one of its kind in Darlington High. It couldn't be swapped for a clarinet or a cornet. But it had spent all this term and last term being unique. Nothing new there.

The reason it mattered *now* was because of what it meant to everyone around it.

Imogen's family expected her to pass her exam on it this afternoon. Everyone knew they were pushy.

Imogen had lost it. Someone had taken it to show her how much she was hated in her class. That was big.

Worse still, the teachers were on the case. Blindly, blunderingly, but definitely on the case. They weren't going to give up until someone had been punished because of it.

It was just a black box with a bit of former tree inside it. But right now there was so much hearts-and-minds stuff packed with it that it might have been a bomb. One way or another, between now and five o'clock, it was going go off. Which would be tough for pretty well everyone. Especially for whoever was holding it at the time.

Unless . . .

Unless Sally could change what it meant.

Unless she could change it from a message of hate to a message of love.

For example, by returning it not just as a case with an oboe inside it, but as a case with an oboe inside it around which was wrapped a piece of folded card with a heart drawn upon it, and in carefully disguised letters, the words I LOVE YOU.

And now the bomb was not a bomb any more. It was a cupid's arrow.

It was a *white* lie, thought Sally guiltily. It was a false trail. It suggested a completely different reason for the disappearance of the oboe. Not a bitchy attempt to put a spoke in Imogen's music career, but a secret admirer, who had stolen it just so that he could return it with a love note. Nothing to do with Billie or Ameena. Nothing to do with the war.

It lowered the stakes. If things went wrong and some boy got caught with it, the worst that would happen to him would be some sharp words and a bit of embarrassment. But if it worked, the teachers would slouch back to their lairs with knowing smiles and shakes of the head. Imogen would be left in a world not of secret enemies but of secret admirers. She'd have something to think about that wasn't Cassie-and-Viola. For all Sally knew, she might put in an inspired performance this afternoon and get a distinction from her examiner. And in all the confusion that would follow, maybe all the problems among the girls would have a chance to die down a bit.

Maybe.

Anyway, it was the only way that Sally could think of to get the oboe back without pointing the finger of guilt at Janey or Billie or anyone like that, because that would just make things worse. Boys did have their uses sometimes. All she needed was one who would deliver it.

And whoever he was, the poor sap wasn't going to get told what was in it either. There was too much riding on this. He'd have to accept his fate and be grateful. Cupid didn't give you the vote.

She was lurking round a corner within sight of the door to the boys' changing room. She had the oboe in her P.E. bag. She was waiting for the football club to finish getting dressed after their lunch-time training. One of them would do.

The changing room door opened. Sam Wray came out.

No, thought Sally.

The door opened again. Jeff Butcher came out, calling over his shoulder to the guys who were still inside.

Again, no, thought Sally.

Why not? Jeff was nice. He'd do it if she asked him.

'It's got to be someone good-looking,' she said to herself.

WINDLEBERRY:	Is that really why you're waiting?
SALLY:	Of course it is.
WINDLEBERRY:	You could deliver it. Just make sure no one sees you.
SALLY:	I can't!
WINDLEBERRY:	Be honest with yourself, Sally. There's another reason you're standing here. Don't you know what it is?

'It's *got* to be a boy,' muttered Sally to herself. She felt quite sure about it. And also, for some reason, angry. And tense. She was trying hard not to panic.

She'd seen Dom. She'd seen Jeff, both Sams, Tim, Tyrone and Louie. And Stevie. She had almost gone for Stevie.

There could only be three of them left in there.

'Come *on*,' she whispered.

The central chamber of Billie's mind was done up like a gothic temple.

(A gothic temple is not a cathedral. Definitely not. It is something quite different and it really exists. In Billie's mind it does anyway.)

The walls were of black stone, rugged and yet shiny, as if this were a cavern underground and the rocks were filmed with chill waters seeping down through the earth. The ceiling was vaulted, the floor uneven, the chamber lit by lamps of crystal set in niches. An eerie wailing came from somewhere. It might have been mystic chanting, but in fact it was Cindy Platter's latest being played over and over through hidden speakers. In the centre of the chamber was a great stone altar block and on it Billie lay like a sacrificial victim, because that was what she wanted to be.

Ismael took out the golden arrow and lifted it high. He was not at ease with the situation. Yeah, sure, if he had to be a priest, then he could be a priest. Organized religion comes naturally to angels.

It was just that he had never expected to be *this* kind of priest.

On the far side of the altar Scattletail looked even more uncomfortable. That was because of his white robes, which were clean.

'Drive it into my heart!' cried Billie.

Ismael sighed. 'You're really up for this, aren't you, honey?'

'I like it.'

'We, um, doin' it now?' said Scattletail. 'Don't we have to wait for someone to, er, come along?'

'Anyone you like,' said Billie, 'provided he's good-looking.'

'What about the Tony bloke?'

'I don't mind if it's him again. But there might be someone better.'

'Like who?'

'Could be anyone,' said Billie. 'Provided he's tall and trim and a bit muscly, tanned skin, dark eyebrows and curly dark hair – an afro, maybe.'

Ismael and Scattletail looked at each other. Billie's *could be anyone* was sounding a lot like Zac Stenton.

'Or blond,' said Billie. 'And he doesn't have to be tall-tall, so long as he's good at sports and has got a lean face and chin.'

And that was Alec Gardner.

Scattletail coughed. 'A lot of scope, there. Lot of room for manoeuvre, you might say.'

'Couldn't we keep it to Year Nine?' pleaded Ismael. 'We'd see so much more—'

'Not on your life,' said Billie. 'The Year Nine boys are all hopeless. I want someone I can be proud of and who will bring me liquorice.'

Ismael tested the arrow with his finger. It was loaded, all right. There was enough power there to make his princess fall in love with any passing frog (or Year Nine) no matter what her wish-list was beforehand. Good job *he* was the one who was holding it . . .

Scattletail must have read his thoughts. As if by magic, a pack of cards appeared in his hands. 'Guess we cut?' he said, grinning evilly.

'Cut?' Ishamel grimaced. 'Not with *your* deck.'

'We'll play for it,' said Billie, promptly sitting up. 'Deal me in.'

'Sure, Queenie.' sighed Ismael. 'You're the boss. What game?'

'Hearts, of course.'

Come on, thought Sally. Come on. Come . . .

The handle of the boys' changing room turned.

Oh no! thought Sally.

Here they come!

Here they came, Zac and Alec and Tony. Three rangy forms, lightly swathed in half-buttoned shirts and loose ties, grinning to each other about something one of them had just said. The air of gods was about them.

And Sally's knees were trembly as she stepped out

into their path. Her palms prickled and her heart was going thump and she wanted to swallow. Nerves, she thought. Just nerves. *Why am I so nervous?*

'Um . . . hi,' she said.

Alec passed her and he hadn't heard.

'Hi,' said Sally again.

Tony 'Hi-Hi'd back. Though Sally wasn't sure he knew who had spoken to him.

'Hi, Sally,' Zac said.

Zac was nice, but he hadn't stopped walking.

They were walking by her, going somewhere she wasn't. If she let them.

'*Um* . . .' she said.

Zac stopped. So did Tony.

Alec looked back. Then he stopped too.

Zac and Alec and Tony.

They were looking at her.

'So this,' said the Angel of Love, 'is where I take over.'

Love can strike like lightning. She can leap out of a rosebush, yelling and firing gold tipped arrows. She can pluck all the fibres of the human soul and make them sing like the strings of a harp. But she doesn't have to.

She can wait.

She can wait like one of those beautiful, carnivorous flowers – the sort that beckons insects and spiders into its sweet-smelling petals (ever thought why it's called the *Venus* flytrap?) and then catches them there.

She waits, standing silently, while the busy little creature goes left and right and up and down, following what it thinks are its own purposes. Until it persuades itself that there's a reason, a very good reason, why it should go to one particular place, alone.

And say, 'Um . . .'

And push forward, into the soft, yielding, deadly embrace.

Sally stood, open-mouthed, lost in the middle of her own mind. Two cupids had caught Muddlespot from behind and wrestled him silently to the floor. About twenty had dropped out of nowhere on top of Windleberry and buried him under a squirming mass of naked bodies, which shuddered sporadically and emitted the occasional muffled *Hai!* but nothing to any effect.

And before her, tall and slim and lightly clad, stood Eros himself. He held a mask in front of his face. Through the eye-holes she felt his gaze burning into her, all the way down to her heart.

Everything stood still.

'Did you know the world is about to end?' said Eros softly. 'It's going to end very soon,' he added. 'A star will fall and everything will burn. Sally, you will burn with it.'

His words burned as he spoke them, and at the same time they sang. Sally nodded slowly. She believed him at once but she did not feel very upset. After all, it hardly mattered. How could anything matter, except him?

'You haven't very long, I'm afraid,' Eros said. 'Not long at all. Time is precious. What do you want to do with it?'

There was a pause.

'Schoolwork?' he said. 'Really?'

Another pause.

'Or save the world? Nice thought. But it can't be saved. Not this time. These days are all you have . . . they are all you have, Sally,' he said. 'So what do you think you are here for?'

Sally could not answer.

'Let's play a little game,' said Eros. 'You'll see what I mean. Let them up.'

The cupids lifted Muddlespot to his feet. They stood behind him, holding his arms. Slowly the pile on top of Windleberry rearranged itself. Windleberry's head and shoulders appeared, poking out of the masses of pinky flesh.

'Let them up,' Eros said again. 'They won't fight. She won't allow it. Will you, Sally?'

'No,' whispered Sally.

Grimly, Windleberry climbed to his feet. His suit was rumpled. There was a bruise on one cheek. Some cupid had remembered the last time they had met and had put the heel in. He folded his arms and faced Eros.

'Game?' he said.

'A very old game,' said Eros sweetly. 'But a good one. We each offer Sally what we have to offer, and then she will choose between us.'

'And the winner?'

'The winner wins.'

'Don't listen, Sally!'

'A disappointing opening,' sighed Eros. 'Amateur, really. I had expected better from you, my dear.' He turned to Muddlespot. 'Would you like to try next?'

Muddlespot opened his mouth and shut it. He knew the game all right. Everyone from Below and Above knew *this* game.

He just hadn't seen it played three-sided before. That was what was throwing him. Suddenly there were a lot more angles and he couldn't work them all out fast enough.

'Do be quick,' said Eros mildly. 'The world *is* about to end, you know.'

Muddlespot panicked. 'All the kingdoms of the world and their splendour,' he gabbled, going straight to his bottom line. 'If you will only bow down and worship me!'

'Ah, the "Wilderness Gambit",' said Eros happily. 'So nice to see it played in the classic manner. *Un*fortunately, the lease on those kingdoms is about to expire very soon. Along with everyone in them. It's not your fault – well, it *is* your fault, as it happens, but don't let that bother you. It's just that if a kingdom is about to go up in smoke, then maybe it isn't really so worth having after all, is it . . . ?

'. . . So, Sally. Shall we think about it? Shall we think about what you *really* want?'

The mask turned in his hand, in one neat movement. It became his face, and it was the face of Alec Gardner. He smiled at Sally, a beautiful, white-toothed smile, and her heart went *thump!*

'Well?' said Alec.

Sally's mouth was dry. 'Let's . . . let's play again,' she managed to say.

The mask twirled in the fingers of Eros. Once more it was as blank as the face of a statue. He turned it on Muddlespot.

'Do you want to improve your offer?'

'Eeeeerrrrrrrhhh . . .' said Muddlespot.

'I don't think you can, can you? Once you've offered all the kingdoms, there aren't any more to offer. Awkward for you.' He turned to Windleberry. 'Would you like to go next?'

'Sally!' Windleberry's voice was urgent. 'You mustn't think about yourself. Think about Truth. The difference between what is True and not True is the only thing worth knowing . . .'

'Ah, wisdom!' said Eros. '*That's* better. I thought we should drag it out of you eventually. And what can I possibly say to that?'

The mask twirled in his hand. It became his face, and it was a living one. Lean, brown, curly-haired. Tony stood in the middle of Sally's mind. He gave an embarrassed shrug. 'Except this?' he said, and grinned. Sally's heart trembled.

'Sally!' cried Windleberry. 'Remember what happens! Remember the play and the city that burned!'

'Hey!' said Tony. 'How was that my fault?'

'What about Ameena's ankle?' said Muddlespot,

who could play the blame game better than any angel. '*That* was because of you!'

♩'Guilty♪!' cried the oboe case from somewhere.

'All right, then,' said Eros, twirling his blank mask in his hand. 'Shall we have one more try? Who are you, Sally? In your heart, who are you? Who are you *for*?'

The mask seemed to slow as he spun it. Sally felt a tingling just below her ribs. It seemed to lift her, as if she had no weight at all. Which was just as well, because her knees were shaking. They had no strength. Her blood was water. Or maybe it was fire. Something in her chest felt as if it was about to burst. She knew who was coming. They all did.

'Riches!' shrieked Muddlespot desperately.

'Wisdom!' cried Windleberry.

'Love,' whispered Eros, putting the mask to his face.

'Anyone want a burger?' said Charlie B.

'Um, what?' said Sally. She had hardly heard him. Zac's face was looking down on her. For an instant that might have been a hundred years she had not been able to think or say anything. Thoughts reeled in her brain like snatches from dreams, without start or finish or sense. Where am I? Here. Where is here? Looking up at Zac. Who is looking at me.

Except he wasn't looking at her. Something else had caught his attention.

'Burger?' he said.

Charlie B had joined them in the corridor. He had three foam burger cases in a stack in his hands.

'My birthday. My brother brought a load to the school gates. These are left over.'

'Hey, cheers,' said Alec, taking one.

'Cheers,' said Tony. He took one too.

Zac hesitated. He looked at Charlie B. He looked at Sally. 'You want a burger, Sally?'

Sally said 'Um . . .'

Tony lifted his burger from its case. There was a smell. Burgers always smell.

But . . . like that?

And far away, a voice from the calendar corridors of her mind shrieked, *It isn't Charlie's birthday!*

'Just check they're the kind you like,' said Charlie offhandedly.

Tony paused, his mouth already open. He lifted the top half of his burger. Charlie grabbed Sally by the arm. Within, Muddlespot grabbed her too.

Both yelled, 'RUN!'

Tony screamed.

17: THE HOUNDS OF HEAVEN

Charlie yanked Sally half off her feet. She staggered and nearly fell. The boys jumped back. The burgers fell from their hands, spilling green and leggy contents that hit the floor with soft plops and – this was the worst – *hopped* when they got there. Alec let out a yell.

'Come *on!*' yelped Charlie, although really he had not needed to say this because the two of them were already halfway down the corridor and accelerating fast.

'You . . . what did you . . . ?' gasped Sally.

'Just *run!*'

'Get them!' roared Zac.

'Get them!' roared Eros in Sally's mind.

'Just—' began Muddlespot.

'I know,' moaned Sally. 'Run!'

They bolted together through the arched doorway

253

that led from the central chamber. An arrow, wickedly tipped with gold, flew past them. Behind her Sally could hear the voices of Zac, the voice of Eros, calling. She fled him down the labyrinthine ways of her mind.

'Fifteen . . . minutes . . . to the . . . bell,' gasped Charlie B. 'Need to . . . get out of . . . sight . . .'

They careered down the English corridor, crashed through the double doors and took the corner at full speed with their feet slipping on the linoleum floor.

'*Hey!*' cried Sam Gosling, as they barged past him.

'What the . . . ?' fumed Amelia, as they kicked over her bag and scattered her books along the floor.

'Sorry!' yelled Sally, disappearing in the direction of the library.

'Hey!' wailed the thoughts in the war rooms as Muddlespot and Sally tore through it, upsetting the tables and sending charts of climate change fluttering through the air. 'What about *us*?'

'Need to . . . think again . . . anyway . . .' Sally gasped. 'If there's an . . . asteroid . . .'

'What?' said the thoughts.

'Tell you lateeerrrrr!' cried Sally, receding in a red blur.

Into the war room burst the cupids, cooing and hallooing, trumpets high and harps waving menacingly.

And all those cool-headed, world-saving ideas, all those Plans and Appeals and Calculations of the Carbon Cycle and Good Resolutions Not to Have Too Many Hot Baths, took one look, shrieked and scattered, as such thoughts always must before the power that rules the human soul.

Deliberate speed! Majestic instancy! The golden hunt poured through the halls of Sally's mind. Horns blew, arrows flew. The corridors heaved and twisted. The crystal columns coloured pink and purple and gold, like trees that catch the sunset. Thoughts wailed and clung to one another, cowering in corners as the cupids passed. Sally and Muddlespot fled before them. As they flew down a corridor, a memory of Greg wandered aimlessly out of a room ahead of them.

Greg! I was going to tell him he had to . . .

The thought of Greg looked around, wide-eyed, intact for just an instant. Then it shattered in a hail of badly-aimed golden arrows and disappeared under a tonne of rose petals. And all the while the voice of Eros beat upon Sally's ear.

'They've . . . split up . . .' puffed Charlie B. 'Gone round the quad . . . to catch us. What are you . . . ?'

Sally had her mobile out of her pocket and was frantically pushing buttons. 'Got to . . . remind

Greg . . . get flowers for Mum,' she panted.

'You . . . crazy!'

'No! Must do this . . . *now*!'

'There they are!'

'Aaaaaaargh!' cried both Sally and Charlie, as Alec appeared in the corridor ahead of them. They swerved to the right and pounded up the stairs. Little showers of invisible stray arrows poured from Sally as she ran. One caught Viola as she loitered haughtily on the landing with her bag over her shoulder. She barely saw Charlie and Sally. She had just time to register Alec pounding up the steps towards her before something thrilled in her heart and she knew that she cared nothing for Tony or Billie or even for standing around looking haughty, but only for flinging herself into his arms, which she did. Both duly fell back down the stairs.

The pursuit tore around the top floor of the school. Miss Tackle and Mr Kingsley, sitting one in his classroom and the other in the staff room, heard the noise. They rose from their seats and came out to restore order, Miss Tackle towering like a thundercloud and Mr Kingsley slithering like an offended snail. They emerged at the exact moment that Sally passed emitting invisible gold arrows in all directions. They saw Sally. They saw each other. Their eyes met.

Mr Kingsley felt sudden confusion. All at once the riot seemed distant. There was chaos and disorder going on somewhere, but strangely it did not matter. The air was a haze of golden things. The face of Theodora Tackle swam before him, a face he had seen every day and yet had somehow always failed to see before this. He had no idea what was happening to him or what he could do about it. He couldn't speak. He didn't dare. He couldn't possibly bring himself to address her. She was an angel, an image of perfection . . .

So it was just as well Miss Tackle looked at him and decided on the spot that she didn't want to be 'Miss Tackle' any more. After that, there was only one way things were going to go.

Still the hunt rioted down the corridors and the golden voices hallooed in Sally's mind, more instant than the feet that were pounding themselves to inch-thin tenderness on the floors of Darlington High.

'Oi-oi-oi-oi!!! There they go!!!!'

'Run!' screamed Muddlespot.

'Run!' screamed Charlie.

And Sally wailed 'But what if I *want* to get caught?'

'It's not worth it,' panted Muddlespot. 'Trust me!'

*

There was a place, at last, where the world stood still. Unlike all the other places in Darlington High, unlike the tossing and disordered passages of Sally's mind, *this* place, strangely, strangely, did not go tumbling off anywhere to become somewhere else.

It was the very unromantic and slightly smelly corner behind the bike sheds to one side of the main parking area. Sally and Charlie sat against a concrete wall and tried to remember how to breathe.

'I think we lost 'em,' panted Charlie, who (given the chance) would always talk in lines from certain kinds of film.

'What was . . . (gasp) in those burgers?'

'Frogs,' said Charlie. 'Got them . . . biology lab . . .'

'You . . .' Sally gagged. '*Charlie!*'

'Ta-daaahhh!'

'But . . .' (gasp) 'they'll think . . .' (gasp) 'I was part of that!'

'You were. You said to give one to Tony.'

'I said forget it!'

'Oh, I *knew* you didn't mean that bit.'

'But . . . Alec and Zac . . .'

'Had to do three. Tony'd have been suspicious if I'd just picked him out.'

Goodbye, Zac, thought Sally sadly. To you, I shall

always be the girl who set you up for a frogburger.

She drew another breath.

Oxygen starvation did funny things. It dulled pain of all kinds. The fact that she would now have to spend the next year and a bit trying *not* to get seen by the three coolest boys in the school seemed, strangely, to be less impossibly dreadful than it should have been. At least, that was how it felt when compared to her immediate and overwhelming need to swallow more air.

She checked her watch. She was astonished to find that there was another ten minutes before the end of break. She felt she had been running for ever.

'Coast's clear,' said Charlie, peering round the corner of the shed. 'No one – uh – Mr Singh's up in the Physics lab. He's looking out of the window.'

Sally's heart bumped harder. Her stomach detached itself and whisked off into some void or other. Her hand was still clutching Imogen's oboe case. She had almost forgotten it was there.

(♩'Guilty♪,' it said to her.)

'What's he doing?' she asked nervously.

'Having a lurk, I guess.'

'He'll be looking for someone with an oboe case.'

Charlie's eye fell on it. 'Ah. And what happens if

259

he finds them?'

Sally shrugged miserably. 'The world will end.'

'We have to lie low for a bit,' said Charlie, reverting to film script.

All right, thought Sally bitterly. I'm guilty. And the guys I thought were cool aren't cool. There was something mean about the way they chased us . . .

And in just a few minutes I'm going to have to walk out and let Mr Singh see me with the oboe and put the cuffs on me. Because Imogen's got to have it back. And then I'll have to lie and take the blame, or tell the truth and get a whole lot of others into trouble. Either way, it's going to be pretty world-ending stuff.

Where's a meteorite when you really want one?

Charlie said, 'Uh-oh.'

Zac and Tony had appeared around the corner of the school.

18. CHARLIE'S LAST STAND

'Keep down,' said Charlie. 'Maybe they'll miss us.'

Again this was film talk. It really didn't matter whether they lay down or stood on tip-toe. The sheds hid them no matter what. So long as no one came round the corner and found them there.

Except that they also needed to see. If they could see, they would know whether to stay put or retreat around the other side of the bike sheds when the sixth-formers came looking. So Sally crammed herself right up close to the corner, made herself as small as possible and peeped with just three quarters of an eye round it so that she could—

She jerked back in alarm. 'They're heading this way,' she hissed.

'They don't know we're here!'

261

Another look. Tony was still coming straight towards them. Zac was angling towards the far corner of the sheds, as if to cut off their retreat. The boys approached slowly, menacingly, like wolves who expected their prey to break into a last, hopeless flight.

'They know.'

They must have seen them from an upstairs window. Something like that. Or someone had told them . . .

'They can't do anything with old Singh out there.'

'They can if we stay put,' said Sally. She hefted the oboe. 'And if we run, and Mr Singh sees me with this . . .'

If she was caught with the oboe it would be Sally in the dock, no mercy, no appeal. Plus Charlie had spread live frog all over the games corridor. Janitors would be screaming. Deputy Heads would have fits. Right now.

And it was her fault. Partly it was anyway.

Guilty, again.

'We'll fight to the last man!' said Charlie.

'Good plan – then what?'

'Then we escape and become mercenaries!'

'Charlie, for *crying* out loud . . . !'

'OK, better plan. Give me that thing.'

His hand was out for the oboe. A strange light had crept into his eyes.

'But . . . it's got to go back to Imogen!'

'Sure. Now give. And stay down.' He took it from her. Before she had time to think, he trotted swiftly around the near end of the bike sheds.

Stay down? She couldn't! He'd gone out there like a robin that thought it could fight crows. Maybe he thought the oboe case really did hold a bomb and he was going to try to use it. Some disaster was only seconds away!

She peered once more round the corner. She saw Charlie start to run. Gathering speed, he burst into the open just as Tony was covering the last metres towards the bike shed. At once he swerved and, uttering a high-pitched yell (with added Doppler effect) he tore past the oncoming sixth-former and charged across the playground towards the school buildings.

'Hey!' yelled Tony, and gave chase.

'Hey!' bellowed Zac, doing ditto.

'EEEE-EEEE-EEEE-EEEE-EEEE-EEEE-EEEEE!' went Charlie, his cry following him like the jet-trail of a ground attack aircraft.

Mr Singh leaned from his window. He saw the hunters. He saw their quarry.

He saw what the quarry was carrying.

'CHARLES BLATCHLEY!' he roared.

Most pupils at Darlington High, addressed by such authority, could be relied on to come dutifully, if guiltily, to heel. Charlie, moving at speed with his mind full of jet fighters and mercenaries, could be relied on with 100% certainty to accelerate. Sally knew this.

So when she saw him skitter to a sheepish halt under Mr Singh's window, she saw that he had *meant* to get caught.

Zac and Tony closed in on him from behind, warily. They weren't exactly sure what was going to happen next. The one thing they were sure of was that the troublesome Year Nine was never going to become a Year Ten. Not if they could possibly help it.

'What have you got in that case?' rumbled Mr Singh.

Charlie ham-acted trying to hide it behind his back.

'What is in the case, Zac?'

Alec took the case. He opened it. 'An oboe,' he said, 'with . . .'

A brightly-coloured bit of card fell spiralling to the playground tarmac. Tony put his foot on it. He picked it up. He read it.

'*Oh* my God,' he said. And, grinning, he showed it to Zac.

'"I love you"!' cried Zac. 'Whoa, Romeo!'

Oh, Charlie, thought Sally. I'm so sorry! Not only have I sent you for execution. I've also sold you to every gossip corner in the school. They'll never let you hear the last of this.

Across the courtyard she saw Charlie stiffen. From forty metres away Sally could not actually tell if his face was changing colour. She just knew it would be. He had been ready for interrogation, torture, solitary confinement. He hadn't reckoned on being caught with a pink heart that said *I Love You*.

But he was made of stern stuff, Charlie B. His round form hid the steel of heroes. He squared his shoulders. His chin tilted mulishly. Maybe he hadn't realized how bad the world could be to him. But he was going to take it. He would carry on taking it until the world ran out of ideas.

'You are in deep trouble, Charlie,' said Mr Singh. 'Serious trouble. Tony, bring him up to my office. Zac, take that instrument to Miss Ogle in form 9c. It belongs to Imogen Grey and must be returned to her straight away. Do it now, please.'

'He took frogs from the biology tanks,' said Tony. 'And tried to feed them to us.'

'*Serious* trouble,' repeated Mr Singh after a pause, as if he was lost for words other than ones he had already used. 'Come now, please.'

He closed the window. Silently, the two sixth-formers marched Charlie towards the school entrance. As they entered the porch Tony dropped back a pace and kicked him in the leg, hard. Charlie stumbled. He kept on walking. The school doors closed behind them.

The car park was empty.

It wasn't quite empty, really, because Sally was in it. She was standing in the open about five metres from the sheds. She had been drawn that far out of hiding by the scene beneath the school windows. No one had looked her way. No one had seemed to think that it was worth looking for anyone else. They had caught Charlie. He was enough of an explanation for everything.

He was going to get it. He was really going to get it. If it had been just the oboe, that bit of paper might have got him off the worst of it (though he

266

would hate being caught with what she had written). But the stunt with the frogs as well . . . The school was *not* going to see the funny side of this. And Charlie already had a number of previous convictions. This wasn't going to be just another detention. This was going to mean parents getting called, suspension maybe. It was going to be heavy, heavy stuff.

He had got himself caught deliberately.

He had been caught, anyway. With the sixth-formers closing on their hideout and the Head of Year at his window, they had been doomed. He had seen that. What he had done was get *her* out of it. He had taken it all on himself.

Why? If you were going to get caught, wasn't it better to get caught *with* someone, so they could share the blame? But Charlie hadn't thought like that. He had taken it all – kicks, frogs and even the oboe (which was nothing to do with him). That wasn't just cool. That was . . .

Somewhere a bell rang for the end of break. Instinctively her body responded. Her feet carried her towards the school entrance. Her mind was turned inwards, on the memory of Charlie. She saw him ahead of her, scurrying towards these same buildings. The buildings towered over him like the walls of a huge city. The windows looked down upon him, blank-eyed, as if they thought that he didn't belong. As if he were a creature from some other place, disguised, who should be expelled as soon as his true nature became clear.

He had seemed so small.

He had done it for her.

And . . .

'*Look out!*' shrieked Muddlespot, far too late.

A sudden image filled her mind, as if she had turned a corner and found something large and round and heavy and gold coming at her very very fast . . .

You would have thought . . .

(thought the Inner Sally, with a sense of flying through space)

. . . that

if

someone

had

parked

a

wrecking

ball

in

my

brain . . .

(*Upmh!* as she came to the ground and saw stars)

. . . I might have *known* it was there?

19: THE END OF THE WORLD (AGAIN)

'There's going to be an investigation,' said Windleberry.

A sort of calm had returned to Sally's mind. The golden hunt had vanished. The corridors and hallways were straightening themselves out again, with a trembly uncertainty as if they weren't sure they would be staying that way. Colours still flushed along the crystal walls, but more weakly now. In the war rooms thoughts regrouped, checked over the register, found out who was still missing and which cupboard they were hiding in. Sally and Muddlespot peeped nervously into the central chamber but Windleberry was alone. Even the black oboe case had gone.

'An investigation?' said Sally, a little shakily. 'What does that mean?'

'Things have been happening that should not have happened,' said Windleberry. 'A team of angels will be coming down to find out why. In fact, they're already on their way.'

Sally hesitated. Then she shrugged. 'Fine by me,' she said. 'But I'm not answering any questions I don't want to.'

'And I get immunity,' said Muddlespot firmly.

Windleberry frowned. 'If that's what Sally wants.'

'It is,' said Sally.

'Where did they go?' said Windleberry.

'Who?' said Sally.

'I think he means the little fat guys,' said Muddlespot. 'You know, the ones with the bows and arrows and harps and the, er, wrecking balls and things . . .'

'Oh, them.' Sally paused. 'I guess they ran out of ammunition.'

'By the way,' said Billie, 'I've dumped Tony.'

'Hmm?' said Sally.

'I said I've dumped Tony,' said Billie, pouting. 'Told him so. Found someone better.'

They were on their way out of the school gates with the main flood of Darlington High pupils. Sally was moving slowly. She was checking the crowds for

Charlie B, but he wasn't there. Probably he was in Mr Singh's office getting things said to him. Possibly he was already on his way to see the Head.

She did see Imogen, hurrying after Cassie and Tara who were talking in high fits of giggles that left them dangerously short of breath. Imogen had her oboe case and was looking horrified and embarrassed. So probably someone had told them about the pink heart and who had been carrying it. And Cassie and Tara thought this was hysterically funny, and Imogen did not think it was funny at all. Whatever she was playing for her exam this evening was going to sound a lot like *The Ride of the Valkyries*.

Poor Charlie!

Viola passed, towing Alec by the hand. Alec was looking dazed (and was going to be in *big* trouble with the Year Twelve girls tomorrow). Viola was grinning from ear to ear. She too was going to be hearing from the Year Twelve girls about this, but she didn't care. She even said 'Hi' to the twins as she passed.

Sally counted four, five, *six* other couples all hand in hand. Mr Kingsley and Miss Tackle were getting into Miss Tackle's car. Somewhere some bird was singing its head off.

Birdsong. The war was over. At least until the

Year Twelves got going. Everyone was smiles. The teachers had their victim. And who had taken the fall?

He had.

'Aren't you even *interested?*' said Billie.

'Mm? Oh, yes. Who?'

Billie's eye gleamed in triumph. '*Wouldn't* you like to know . . .'

Not really, thought Sally. The way you're going, you'll be on number three by the end of the week. Or five.

'Tall and handsome?' she sighed.

'Yes to both. Going to guess?'

Sally was looking around again.

'You all right, Sally?'

'Hmm? Oh, I'm fine.'

There was still no sign of him.

The CIA (Celestial Inspections Angel) was huge. He was also humourless. High on the crest of his flaming hair he wore a peaked cap. He took notes by burning the letters into a small tablet of stone with his fingernail.

'. . . deny that I entered the City illegally,' he intoned. 'I deny attempting to obtain controlled store items under false pretences. I deny assaulting a citizen of the City. I deny the charge of theft. I deny the charge of—'

'Ahem,' said Muddlespot. '*You* don't get to charge me with anything.'

'That's right,' said Sally, standing by with her arms folded.

'So mind your manners or I'll bite your kneecaps,' snarled Muddlespot.

The angel looked down. Muddlespot did, indeed, come up to his kneecaps.

'. . . state that I did not impersonate a duly-summoned witness to the Appeals Board . . .' said the angel, ponderously burning out his letters with his fingernail. 'Accordingly I state that the facts contained in the full confession filed by the Guardian Windleberry are false . . .'

'Ahem,' said Muddlespot. 'I think you'll find that what my, er, my colleague over there has filed is not a "confession" but a complaint against another one of your departments . . .'

'That is correct,' said Windleberry.

'Which will be duly investigated,' said the CIA woodenly.

'I have also said that whatever the results of her

examination, I believe Sally now has grounds for Appeal,' said Windleberry.

'Oh,' said the CIA.

'Which will be of interest to my Authorities in due course,' said Muddlespot smoothly. 'In the meantime I am merely, as a professional, responding to your enquiries to the fullest of my professional ability.'

'You mean you're lying with every word,' said the angel.

'Now now,' said Muddlespot.

In the doorway two other angels, clad in white suits, were comparing notes.

'. . . one hundred and twenty golden arrows and other missiles signed out from stores,' one was saying. 'Fifty-six returned. That makes sixty-four fired on the mission . . .'

'. . . and we have thirty-three impact sites within the brain. Fifteen external, plus eleven collateral hits – ten humans and one sparrow. Total fifty-nine. Five still unaccounted for . . .' He looked at Sally, Muddlespot and Windleberry. 'Nobody stopped an arrow without noticing it?'

The three looked at each other. Beyond them the corridors of Sally's mind echoed with murmurs. Teams of angels were carefully picking over debris, interviewing thoughts, examining little chips and marks in the walls. ' . . . *fired from the steps up there. Impact here, ricocheting . . . temporary impairment to the mathematical functions. May not be too serious . . .*'

'Arrows?' said Muddlespot. 'Er no, no arrows. Not this time, anyway.'

'I didn't stop anything,' said Sally with perfect truth.

'Get the stores totals checked,' sighed a CIA. 'It'd be just like the cupids to be sloppy with their paper-work.'

'Have to interview each of the collaterals as well. Statements from every one. And see if there are any others we've missed. Anybody want to try the sparrow?'

'Oh please, not me!'

'Sally?' said Windleberry.

'Hmm?'

'Is there something you haven't told me?'

'I'm totally fine.'

'You know what?' said a CIA. 'The Appeals Board will be going to town on this. They'll abso-lutely go to town.'

Sally's mobile beeped. It was a reply from Greg.

> Thks Sal. Have got her roses. Cost a mint
> but she's worth it.

'Well done, Greg,' Sally murmured. 'You'll live to fight another day.'

'Wossat?' said Billie.

Sally stopped on the pavement.

His bus went at quarter to, she thought. From the shelter just opposite the newsagent. If he had been kept back to see the Head, he'd have missed it. He'd be waiting there now.

And if he wasn't there, maybe he'd be in after-school detention. In which case he'd still be at the bus stop at about quarter to five.

'You go on,' she said. 'I'll be home later.'

'What's the matter?'

'I've – left something behind.'

She turned and started the short walk back towards Darlington High.

It was strange, she thought, how quickly the streets had emptied.

'Charlie B?' said the Angel of Love.

(That's 'said' as in 'about six octaves above normal pitch'.)

The wrecking-ball cupid, who was still wearing his hard yellow hat because it was nice to get a chance to wear anything in his line of work, shuffled his feet on the Floor of Willing Sacrifice. He muttered something.

'Charlie *Beee*???' repeated the Angel of Love. 'We mobilized the *whole* Department, we descended unto Earth with *fate* and *music* and *passion* and what we gave her was *CHARLIE BEEEEEEE*??????'

'You just said to get 'em, Erry,' muttered the cupid.

The Angel of Love leaned forward. She rested her elbows on her desk (which was, of course, still beating). 'Are there *no* professional standards in my Department?' she said, in a dangerous, cold voice.

The cupid hesitated. He wanted to say 'no'. Or did he? 'No' seemed right. It fitted with his cupid's natural desire to deny everything. But he wasn't sure that the double negative would work in his favour.

'We were going to harrow her soul,' said the angel lightly. (So lightly that it was terrifying.) 'Unrequited love, you remember? Fever? Rend the fabric of her being? There's a Guardian there who needs to wish he

278

had never existed! Tell me, sweetie – how are we to do *that* with Charlie B?'

'Could still . . .'

'Charlie B?' sighed Love. 'She'll make him into a safe, reliable chemist in six months.'

The cupid launched a last, desperate defence. 'Er . . . Harrows and fevers an stuff, Erry. Come ter fink of it. 'Snot very *angelic*, is it? Maybe it's just as well we don't—'

Then he looked into his leader's glittering stare and wished he hadn't.

'I am *Love*, my darling,' she whispered. 'Those rules do not apply to me.'

'Sorry, Erry,' said the cupid, who was trying to hide under his hat.

'No, don't be sorry. I think you've just been working too hard. You need a change . . .'

'No, Erry!' pleaded the cupid. 'Please, no . . .'

'. . . Report to my secretary. I believe he's been looking for a replacement.'

'Aiiiiieeeeeeeeee!!!!!'

Bells rang, a sudden chime. The angel picked a golden telephone from her bumping desk. 'Yes?' she snapped.

'It's the Appeals Board, Erry,' said her soon-to-be-relieved secretary's voice in her ear. 'Yer summoned.

They've got ter do an Inquiry into the Jones kid case.'

The angel's eyes hardened. 'Oh, have they?' she said. 'Oh dear. What *shall* we do about that, I wonder!'

'And that great sucking sound you hear,' said Doomsday, 'is the Appeals Board all licking their lips together.'

'They don't have lips,' said a very dejected Mishamh. 'Or if they do, they can't lick them.'

'Metaphorically. Anyway, notice has been given of an Appeal. The case includes entry by an unauthorized person, theft of a restricted item and a number of other things for which there is no precedent. And, of course, the Department of Love is in the thick of it – again. The Board is opening preliminary hearings. They also want to see the candidate's full examination papers . . .'

'But that will take decades,' groaned Mishamh. 'She can hardly have started them!'

'At a guess, she has just reached question two thousand and something.'

'So we'll have to postpone, after all,' said Mishamh gloomily.

'It was a *good* asteroid,' said Doomsday kindly. 'Very neat. Very efficient. Ask it to call back again in, er, in two thousand six hundred years. There's every chance we'll need it then.'

'I just don't understand! How can the Governors allow this? Shouldn't Love just be reined in? What *about* the Curriculum!'

'Mm, yes,' said Doomsday. 'I have a theory about that.'

The bus stop was empty. The pavement outside the school gates was empty. So was the school car park. The windows stared silently at Sally.

She settled down to wait.

'Sir?' said Mishamh. He felt he had nothing to lose now.

'Mm, yes?'

'You said you had a theory, sir.'

'I did say that.'

Doomsday might have left it there. But as archangels go, he was merciful. At least to his staff.

'. . . I think the Governors like things the way they are,' he said.

'But—'

'*Why*, Mishamh? Is that what you were going

to ask?'

Mishamh heard the warning note. He felt the weight of it settle upon his shoulders. He looked up into the eyes of ice.

'Yes . . . yes, sir, it was.'

'*Why* do the Governors, who are entrusted with Heaven, who wrote the Great Curriculum, who make the Laws by which all Creation runs, allow such confusion? *Why*, indeed, is Love a part of the Curriculum at all? I have a theory, but I cannot tell it to you. Can you tell me? Can *you* tell *me* why the Governors allow what they allow?'

'Yes, sir,' said Mishamh with a hollow, tingly feeling in his chest. He nodded slowly. 'Yes, I think I can – now.'

'And that is?'

'It's so they can cheat when they want to.'

Down below them, small and blue and beautiful, turned the world they could never destroy.